matchmaking in progress

Three Player Tag-Team Book 3

allyson lindt

acelette press

For everyone who dares to create

1 /
sonya

"Lady and gentleman, welcome to beautiful Walnut Creek, California," Jeremy boomed in his best announcer-voice, as he navigated the streets. "Fun fact—the city got its name from the trees. When gold rush settlers arrived in July 1957, they needed a way to stay warm during the brutal blizzards, and when they cut firewood, the walnut trees made a unique creaking sound when they fell."

I didn't try to hide my laugh at his ridiculous story. "It's *creek* with two *e*'s, not an *e-a*."

He met my gaze in the rearview mirror. "Why is everyone always hating on EA?"

"You have to ask?"

"I think there are a few more flaws with his story than a spelling error," my roommate, Quentin said from the passenger seat. "Gold rush in 1957? What?"

Jeremy let out a loud sigh and turned down a side road. "There are haters in every group."

"We're not *hating*." Quentin used air quotes. "But if you're going to dump the revisionist history on us, at least warn us first. And really, does your boss know what a horrendous speller you are?"

That was me. His boss. Though Jeremy had seniority in the gaming industry, and most days, there was more teamwork involved than my bossing him around. Since we were the only two writers for the MMORPG we worked on, there wasn't any room for people who didn't put in the hours.

"I do know, and I'm grateful for spell check," I said. "Though, not so much for autocorrect. There was so much *ducking* in his last game script that the art department was arguing over which one of them had to create waterfowl to introduce into the world."

Jeremy rolled his eyes. "Yup. Total haters."

"You're sure you don't mean heaters?" Quentin teased.

"Bite me, leatherneck."

Quentin blew him a kiss. "*Ooh rah.*" He hadn't been enlisted for nearly fifteen years, but once a Marine, always a Marine.

Now that was an interesting thought—Quentin and Jeremy together. I liked that fantasy. "Can I watch?" My love of slashfic—male-slash-male fanfiction—was no secret. It was how I'd gotten my start in the gaming industry. The company that picked me up was looking for a writer who wrote specifically that, to work on one of their top titles, and I'd successfully guessed the future of their game in one of my fanfics.

But the chemistry between Jeremy and Quentin had been heating up since we left on this road trip, leading to daydreams of the two of them fucking that were better than anything I concocted about fictional characters.

My phone rang, and I checked the screen. "It's Megan." I swiped *Answer*. "Hey you."

"*Hi Megan*," Jeremy and Quentin called.

She laughed. "Tell them I said *hi*. How far are you from the hotel?"

We'd discovered this convention in California, and since all of us were single and anti-relationship, we decided a road trip over Valentine's Day weekend—to geek out and not think about love—sounded like a great time. Megan was supposed to come with us, but she'd gotten sick at the last minute.

"Not far. Why?" I asked. It was sweet that she was checking in—she was my best friend and Jeremy's sister, so of course she was concerned—but a phone call wasn't like her.

"So…" She made a series of soft clucking noises. "Some Bookbocker picked up your newest release and said a lot of amazing things about it, and it's blowing up. You've gone viral."

"What?" My brain stalled on the news. I'd been writing fantasy under a penname for years, but it had never made much of a splash. I did it for the love, not the money. "When? We haven't even been on the road for half a day."

"That's all it took."

"What's up?" Quentin asked.

I held up a finger. "You're yanking my chain, right?" I said to Megan. "This didn't... No."

"Seriously. I'm sending you the video link and letting you check in and get settled. This is *amazing* news. Make the guys take you to celebrate."

"Um, okay. Talk soon." I still couldn't believe her. My books didn't *go viral*. I had a small but loyal following, who funded the venture with their enthusiasm, but it was my day job that paid the bills.

Jeremy pulled into the hotel parking lot and trawled for a spot, while I opened up the video Megan sent.

"What'd she say?" he asked.

I relayed her message.

Jeremy parked. "That's *awesome*. Show us." His enthusiasm combined with what lingered from Megan's call and pushed aside more of my doubt.

I leaned forward between the seats of his SUV, held out my phone so all three of us could see, and hit *Play*.

The clip was all text over my book cover. Snippets of the book, interspersed with comments on how hot the different teasers were.

It only lasted about thirty seconds, and when it was finished, Quentin let out a loud *whoop*. "That's fantastic."

"Dustin would kill for those kinds of views and likes." Jeremy pointed at the numbers.

That was when the grin hit, popping onto my face so hard and fast, my cheeks hurt. "It's real. People love my book. Holy shit."

"Because you're brilliant," Jeremy shut off the engine. "Of course they do."

"He's right; you are. Let's check in so we can go celebrate." Quentin grabbed my phone and slipped it in his pocket in a single, flawless move.

I stared at him in disbelief. "What are you doing? Give it back."

"Nope. Because you won't put it down all night if I do. You'll spend the next several hours locked in a doomscroll, reading everything you can find and refreshing when you can't find anything, and then checking your sales numbers for that little hit of dopamine."

Busted. It was the same reason he'd made me promise not to check anything but calls and texts while we were on the road. "Just one look. My book went viral."

"And it will keep going, even if you don't look

for a few hours. Come on." Quentin climbed from the SUV, opened my door, and tugged me to stand on the asphalt.

He was right.

I wanted to look anyway. I lunged for his pocket as he turned away.

"Nope." Jeremy came from nowhere and grabbed my wrist. "He's right."

Quentin snagged my other wrist and stepped in, pressing me back until I was sandwiched between him and Jeremy. "If you want to stick your hand down someone's pants, there's a volunteer behind you."

Jeremy tightened his grip, sending a pulse of want through me. There were days—not many, but it happened—when I let myself entertain the notion of being with either Jeremy or Quentin. When I imagined myself taking the place of one of them in one of my more vivid fantasies.

But guys like this—gorgeous, self-assured, and smart—didn't go for women who were frumpy and spent too much time with their heads in the clouds. Women like me. It was an old insecurity, and probably at least part of the reason I was still single at forty, with no prospects on the horizon, but this was who I was.

I let out an exaggerated sigh. "Fine. I'll behave for now. But you have to distract me with an amazing celebration."

"Of course." Jeremy let go of my hand and tugged the long braid that ran down my back. "Anything for my favorite girl, and this deserves an awesome night."

We grabbed our bags from the back of the truck. There wasn't a lot, since we were only here for two nights, but Quentin insisted on carrying mine as well as his.

The lobby was crowded with an eclectic blend of people in costumes alongside people dressed more conservatively—like us.

Excitement thrummed inside. I loved conventions, and I was riding the euphoria of the *viral* news on top of that. It was going to be hard to sit still tonight.

The line to check in wasn't too bad. Jeremy nudged me toward the available desk clerk.

"Sonya Russel. I have a reservation," I said.

She typed. Frowned. Typed some more. "Can you spell that for me?"

I spelled out my name a letter at a time, and she typed as I talked.

"I'm sorry—you said *Russel?*"

"And *Sonya* with a *Y*, yes." Concern crept inside.

Her frown deepened. "Would it be under another name?"

"Maybe." It shouldn't be, but there had to be some reason she couldn't find me. "My friend Megan Hammond made the original reservation, but she called yesterday to switch it over to my name."

More typing. "No, she called and canceled yesterday."

"No, she didn't. I was sitting there when she made the call."

Quentin's arm brushed mine when he stepped up next to me. "Is there a problem?"

"Someone canceled Megan's reservation instead of switching it to me." I tried to suppress my frustration. This wasn't the desk clerk's fault, but it was irritating.

"So give her a different room." Maybe Quentin's imposing presence would get me further than my meek one.

The desk clerk shook her head. "There are no more rooms. I'm sorry."

"Is mine in the system?" Jeremy joined us as well, and gave her his first and last name. He and Quentin were sharing a room, which would be amazing fantasy fodder if I weren't torn between stress and euphoria.

"Yes," the clerk said.

"Good. Sonya can stay with us." Jeremy looked at Quentin, who shrugged in agreement.

Whew.

Wait.

The gears turned in my head, and any disappointment at my reservation being gone vanished. I gasped at the next thought that entered my head.

Jeremy winced, but he was smiling. "Do you have to say it?"

"I have to say it."

"Excuse me—*say* what?" the desk clerk asked.

Quentin snorted.

"*But there was only one bed.*" One of my favorite romance tropes ever. Sure, this wasn't a romance novel, but I liked when real life matched books even a little.

Both men laughed. They knew me so well.

"There are two beds. It's a double." The desk clerk looked between the three of us, confusion on her face. "And I can send up a roll-away bed as well."

And there was reality, going and being all *real* again.

"Thank you." I kept my smile pleasant.

Quentin nudged me, as we walked toward the elevators. "Just because she doesn't get it doesn't mean we don't. Hands-up if you're secretly harboring a crush for at least one of the other people you *have* to share a room with tonight."

Jeremy's hand shot into the air. "What? I thought this was how the game was played."

"I always knew you cared." Quentin managed to wrap an arm around Jeremy's waist without displacing the bags he carried. He pressed Jeremy to the wall. "Why didn't you say something?"

Jeremy wasn't fazed. "Honestly? Men who are good with their hands intimidate me."

"Interesting insecurity." Quentin let him go.

Jeremy led the way to a waiting lift. "I didn't say that."

"You didn't have to." Quentin's voice shifted to low and seductive.

The two of them dissolved into laughter, as we rode the car up to our floor, but my imagination was whirring again. If I weren't here, would they have hooked up tonight? *Goddess*, I'd like to watch that.

2 /
quentin

We set our bags in our room. It wasn't like sharing a space with Sonya was a new thing, though her place was much bigger than this hotel room. While she didn't tend to wander around the house naked, I always enjoyed catching a glimpse of her in nothing but an oversized T-shirt and panties. Her brown hair falling down her back, the perfect length for pulling. Her long legs on display...

She called me her *roommate*, which was sweet on her part. I was a renter, and she didn't charge me nearly as much as she could.

"Celebration." Jeremy clapped. "Sonya's choice, my treat."

The idea was a good one, but every bit of me wanted to say *our* treat. Two years ago, my husband walked out on me after draining our personal bank account as well as the one that belonged to our contractor business. I'd been left with customers who wanted their work done or their money back, a ruined professional reputation, and bankruptcy. Any money I made from the few jobs I managed to get went to paying someone back for my ex's fucking me over.

Sonya furrowed her brow. "Of course you'd make me pick."

"You're the one who went viral," I said.

"I know." And now her grin was back. "Isn't it weird? Okay. Um... *Oh.* We're near the coast. That means fresh seafood."

"I'll find us a place if you two want to freshen up before we go." At least I could look for restaurants.

We all got ready, and a short while later arrived at our destination, to find a line out the door. Any place would be busy, and since we were here, it made sense to stay.

Half an hour later, when we'd barely made it inside and hadn't even given the host our names yet to secure a table, staying no longer seemed like the best idea.

"We can go someplace else. I don't want to waste everyone's evening." Sonya sounded bummed.

I wasn't having it. "This is your night, and this is what you're in the mood for. Of course we're not going someplace else."

"If she doesn't want to stay, give the bitch what

she wants and get the fuck out of our way." The voice came from behind me.

Fury raced inside me. I'd spent a long time learning to control my temper when I was younger, but times like these, I let my grip slip just a little. I whirled on the man and squared my shoulders. I wasn't small, but neither was he.

He sneered. "Ah. So she's *your* bitch."

The trick was for me to stay cool and collected, but not to let him know that. This kind of asshole needed to know they couldn't just go around saying what they wanted. I pressed my forearm to his throat and pinned him to the wall before he could blink. It was easy to use my weight to lock him in place and apply pressure to his windpipe. "Whose bitch are you?"

"*Fuck you*," he spat.

"I hope they're more eloquent than you are." I stayed cool and removed and pressed in harder.

Another man, thinner and taller, stepped up next to us. "Let's go, man. This isn't worth it."

Bitchman growled and stared me down.

I returned his look with an icy glare.

"Yeah, let's go." Bitchman's implied surrender was enough to make me loosen my grip, but I didn't relax until he climbed into his car. A guy never knew when someone would try to take a sucker-punch swing.

With the irritation gone, I forced calm to return,

and the rest of the world swam back into view. Everyone was staring, including Jeremy. But Sonya was looking at her feet.

Which she would've been doing anyway if the guy had kept up his verbal assault. No one had gotten hurt, and I wouldn't have thrown a punch unless he did. This way, he'd think twice before harassing the next group.

A former Marine buddy had introduced me to Sonya—they used to work together—and the first time I met her, I was enthralled. I was also just coming out of my failed marriage and needing a place to stay, so renting a room from her made more sense than hooking up with her.

Now that I knew her, I was glad I'd made that choice. She deserved more than a one-night stand, and at forty-one, I was too old and jaded to get into any sort of dating game.

But I would protect her for all I was worth, even from simple things like restaurant bullies.

"Excuse me." Three people in matching black vests and slacks approached us. "We've had a complaint and need to ask you to leave."

Seriously?

"Please," Sonya said softly and tugged my sleeve.

I wished she would figure out for herself what her thoughts and time and opinion were worth. "All right."

We all climbed back into the SUV. "Where to?" Jeremy asked.

"The Saturday night before Valentine's Day probably isn't the best time to be trawling a new city, looking for a place that might have seats." Sonya had recovered her voice now that we'd left the lines and confrontation behind. "We should celebrate by picking up food and eating back at the hotel."

I glanced back at her. "How is that special, compared to ordering takeout at home?"

"Because we're calling it a celebration. Also, because someone else has to make the beds and do the laundry in the morning."

Her optimism made me smile. "I'm in."

"Where to?" Jeremy asked again.

We found a place online that was supposed to have *the best burgers in the city* that also had a drive thru, and a short while later, we were back at the hotel.

"Your phone's in my back pocket." I angled toward Sonya on the elevator ride up. "I can't stop you from taking it back if you'd like."

"No. I want to enjoy the night. But you're lucky I trust you with my most precious prosthetic device," she teased.

"You're right; I am." I meant it far more than the light exchange implied. It would be nice to be capable of that level of trust, and if I were, I'd give it to her.

Inside the room, I started to pull out chairs for each of us to sit in, but Jeremy and Sonya arranged the food on one of the beds.

I saw a flaw with their plan. "One of us has to sleep in that bed."

"Easier to share this way," Sonya said.

Jeremy snatched one of her zucchini fries. "We promise to shake any crumbs off when we're done."

Where Sonya was ninety-nine percent kindness and positivity, Jeremy was more like easy going chaos.

We settled on the bed to eat and share food and stories. We each had at least one about some famous person we'd met, who wasn't at all like we expected.

Jeremy told his stories with a lot of flair, though. We were clearing away empty boxes, when he slid into, "So Zach met him at CES in—like—2002, and they hit it off."

"No shit." I was impressed. "Is he as nice as everyone says?"

Jeremy nodded. "Nicer. But back then, no one knew him as anything more than the guy from the runaway-bus movie. He wanted to try voice acting, and we needed a villain for the game."

"No." Sonya's jaw dropped. "You've never told me this. He was the leader of The Hoarde?"

"*Was* being the operative word. He hung out with us for a week in the Cord offices while he recorded his lines, and he was literally the nicest guy ever. Almost as nice as you." Jeremy looked at Sonya. "But when the buy-out happened, he had good enough lawyers that his rights didn't transfer to Digital Media, and they had to remove his voice from everything."

Cool but also bummer. "I would've loved to hear those originals."

Jeremy shrugged. "Pretty sure someone still has a copy of the masters, but I couldn't guarantee who."

"The composer?" I asked.

Sonya grinned. "Checks out. Oh, speaking of Mr. Actor—Rule 34, the *Jack Torch* movies, but everyone is a sex worker *and* an assassin."

"I don't know if that's too easy or too gory for me." Jeremy seemed to be giving this serious consideration.

And I had no idea what they were doing. "*Rule 34?* Isn't that the porn thing?"

Sonya straightened up and interlocked her fingers in front of her, looking like she was about to give a lecture. "Precisely. Rule 34 states that if something exists, there's porn of it on the internet."

"And the game is to pick a movie or TV show and figure out what kind of porn either exists about it or should," Jeremy said. "They're pretty loose rules. But I'm nixing *Jack Torch*. If I'm watching gore porn, I want it to be because of a horror movie, and not because there's actual sex involved."

That seemed reasonable. "Everyone has their limits."

"*But*"—Jeremy leaned into the word—"age the characters up to college, and I'll vote for Harry Potter. Lots of potential for magic wands."

Sonya sighed and rolled her eyes. "Also overdone. It's like you're not even trying."

I still wasn't sure I understood the rules, but the subject was the perfect segue, especially since Jeremy had brought up the gaming company he got his start with. This was an opportunity to ask something I'd been wondering about for a long time. "Is it true you guys used to have honest-to-God orgies back in the day?"

"No subtlety or lead-in there." Surprise tinged Sonya's amusement. "Just *bam. Orgies.*"

"I don't assume they just happen." I shoved the rest of our trash in a bag and set it aside. "I figure they take a lot of planning."

Jeremy stretched his legs out into the now empty space in front of him on the bed. "Yes, but also no?"

"To the planning or that they actually happened?" Sonya asked.

He nodded. "Yes."

I couldn't even fathom. Rather, I could imagine an orgy just fine—*thanks, porn*—but it didn't seem like the kind of thing that would work in real life. "How's that work, then?"

"First time, it was totally spontaneous," Jeremy

said. "A handful of us were celebrating after a long push to meet a deadline. We'd spent weeks in a room together, and the tension wasn't fading as fast as we'd like. A couple of us were to the point of *fuck or fight*."

Sonya grinned. "I bet Brandon initiated it."

"Thin guy with glasses? The singer?" I couldn't picture it.

"Composer," Jeremy corrected me. "And yes, Brandon frequently started it."

I felt like I was at a disadvantage. "So Sonya knows this story."

"Not this bit, I don't. No one talks about the past in detail; they all just say it happened. If you weren't there, you don't know."

That movie, I'd seen. "Like *Fight Club*?"

"Yes, but also no." Jeremy seemed to be enjoying drawing this out. I bet he was a hell of a tease in the bedroom. "It's not that anyone is hiding the past, but most of them have moved on, and no one wants to hear stories about other people having sex." He knew better.

"I do." Sonya grinned.

"That's literally what the two of you do for a living. Tell stories about other people having sex." Not that I needed to remind them.

Jeremy's self-satisfied smirk grew. "Like I said, we'd just finished a huge deadline, and of course back then, the files had to be pressed to CD and planning on Day One updates wasn't realistic, so the game was perfect when we sent it out the door."

"Let's be honest. It wasn't *perfect.*" Sonya dragged the word out.

"Do you want to hear the story or not?"

She pouted. "Yes please."

"Picture this—we'd been geeks and outcasts most of our lives, and we'd finally found our tribe, who we'd spent every waking hour with for months, shoulder to shoulder, because that was all the space we had. We'd been living off pizza, Dew, and stress, and then tension plummeted."

I didn't know if all of the backstory was necessary, but it did help build a mood and its own kind of tension.

"Link—one of the developers—made a comment about needing to get a punching bag or something installed in the break room," Jeremy said. "Nigel wanted a dart board. Phillip said we just needed to get laid."

I couldn't put faces to most of the names he was spitting out, and I'd be lucky to keep their personalities straight for the length of the story, but I appreciated the detail more the longer Jeremy talked.

"And Brandon said"—Jeremy looked at each of us, and time ticked by—"*last one is easiest. No purchase required.* Elliot argued maybe that was true for the pretty creatives, and Brandon kissed him."

Sonya clapped. "I knew it."

Her glee was almost better than the story itself, which... How much of what Jeremy said was real? If I found myself in a situation like that, would I act? Take a kiss from the adorably sweet Sonya? No. I'd want to, but the situation wouldn't change my resolution to keep her at a distance.

Jeremy, on the other hand... He might be a lot of fun to back into a corner and steal a kiss—or more—from.

3 /
jeremy

I was an incredible storyteller, but I preferred them to be other people's stories. Diving into my past—my divorce and what came before it—was messy for me. It had been years, and I still regretted the way my marriage ended.

And I hated that regret.

Besides, these were stories about people I still worked with and all the meaningless sex we had years ago. That was weird, wasn't it?

It didn't matter, because Sonya's happiness when I dove into the story was worth every second and made it easy for me to focus on the words and set regret aside.

My sister, Megan, had made me swear on multiple occasions to never hit on Sonya, and I agreed with her reasons—I didn't want to infect Sonya with my cynicism—but that didn't stop me from enjoying her company and the scenery.

"Keep in mind," I continued, "that like any tech company at the time, we didn't have an equal ratio of men to women." And one of those women now owned the company we worked for. Definitely something weird about including her in stories about sex. "And most of us were the kinds of geeks who had limited experience with the opposite sex. We definitely didn't realize we were interested in the same sex as well."

Talk about eye-opening revelations. "But Brandon's initiating that first kiss, that first grope—not that Elliot was complaining; he was totally feeling back—broke down a lot of walls. Suddenly, the bolder guys were kissing the shyer ones. The women were kissing each other. Us. It was a flurry of limbs and lips and nakedness."

And remembering another guy's hand wrapped around my cock for the first time. It wasn't my first kiss with a girl, but I'd never had one shove my fingers inside her before. The memories raced with heat through my veins and tugged at my desire.

"*Limbs and lips and nakedness?*" Quentin's disbelief interrupted my thoughts but didn't make me go limp. "You know more descriptive language than that."

"*Fingering and fucking?*" Sonya offered.

More direct, but not necessarily more descriptive.

Quentin's snort said he agreed. "And I know *you* know better. I've read your books."

"But I wasn't there." Sonya was one of the newer additions to the group of people I'd worked with through three companies now. She was brought in to Rinslet to pick up the slack when the previous head writer was promoted so far up the chain, she couldn't do the writing anymore.

Quentin looked at me. "Then you're going to have to step up your game. If you're going to talk about orgies, I want details."

"I charge extra for dirty-talk." I didn't really—I was more of a slut than a whore—but I was already turning myself on, and getting explicit would only amplify that. Unless this was going to turn into a three-person recreation, I wasn't interested in dragging out this hard-on.

Quentin leaned back and stretched out his legs. "I'll let you watch me jerk off while you talk. How's that for payment?"

That escalated quickly. "You're not going to feel awkward, being the only one beating your meat?"

"I spent two years sharing living quarters with men who had no concept of personal space. I don't care who does or doesn't join in, as long as no one minds that I'm doing it." Quentin's retort was the embodiment of *casual challenge*.

I'd like to say I didn't rise to the occasion, but the exchange was as much of a turn-on as dipping my toes into my past was. There was still the matter of the third person in the room, though.

I looked at Sonya. We weren't talking about sex, just masturbation. That wasn't the same as hooking up at all, and the number of times I'd fantasized about watching her, touching her, watching her touch herself… "What say you?"

"If you're both doing it, I'm in. So much easier than sneaking into the bathroom later, hoping everyone is asleep and trying to keep quiet."

That was hot too. Especially the idea of catching her, and her not stopping.

"Just to get the obligatory stuff out of the way," Quentin said. "We do this, and no one feels guilty or awkward in the morning."

"I never feel bad about a good wank." I adjusted myself so I had easier access.

Bottom lip caught between her teeth, Sonya studied us and stripped off her shirt. *Fucking hell*, she was wearing a cotton comic-book bra in red and black, and that made the entire situation even hotter.

"But you have to keep telling the story," Sonya said.

How was I supposed to turn down a request like that? Especially when she licked her lips, leaving a kissable shine behind?

"I had limited experience with women at the time." I didn't have a problem admitting that—

everyone started somewhere. "And I hadn't yet admitted to myself in any way that I was bisexual."

"Who was your first?" Sonya asked.

I didn't need her to clarify that she meant *first guy*. It was easy to look back on this and view the physical without an emotional attachment, because there wasn't one at the time. "Elliot." No one ever expected the quiet ones—particularly the ones who looked nerdy. "He smashed his mouth to mine and shoved his hand down my pants to stroke my cock."

The way Sonya bit her bottom lip was the perfect visual to go with Quentin's groan.

And I was eating up this audience of two. "So he's got his tongue down my throat, and I'm trying to return the favor while he jerks me off, and he stops. *Bam.* Leaves me hard and whimpering, with my dick hanging out. Then he unzips his pants and pushes me to my knees." I learned a lot of things about myself back then. Like that I was happy taking charge or letting someone else do so. "The dick he shoves in my face is big enough to choke on."

Was this really what I wanted to be talking about? It was a scorching memory, but Quentin stroking his cock was *now*. Sonya unzipping her jeans to reveal anime panties that had nothing to do with her bra was so much better than diving into my past.

She kneaded round breasts that were the perfect

26

size to fit in my hand, and he slowly moved his hand up and down his shaft. He was at least as big as Elliot, and probably at least as demanding.

No one suspected the quiet ones.

"Is there more to the story?" Sonya asked.

"There is, but that's in the past."

Quentin raised his brows. "I was promised dirty-talk."

I wouldn't mind wrapping my lips around his cock, and Sonya loved a good guy-kissing-guy story or visual. Her being turned on by our turning each other on? That sounded like a lot of fun. I rolled onto my knees and crawled toward Quentin, who watched me with a mixture of surprise and curiosity.

If he wanted dirty-talk, I could deliver. "I want you to fuck my face." Being versatile and knowing how to ask for what I wanted served me in a large number of situations. "I want you to use me as your own personal cum bucket and tell me when I can get off."

Sonya's whimper made me harder.

Quentin held my gaze, searching my face. He knotted his fingers in my hair and guided my mouth onto his cock. "Not sure how you're going to talk with your mouth full, but I like what you've said already."

There would be more talking soon enough.

I sucked and licked, tasting skin and sweat and

precum. Quentin kept one fist tangled in my hair and the other wrapped around his shaft, stroking himself while he set the pace for me.

Sonya's sighs became moans, and Quentin's grunts grew more punctuated.

Just like in my story about the past, my dick was hanging out and begging for attention, but I was too focused on holding myself up while Quentin thrust against my face, to do anything about my own arousal. It was painfully delicious.

Sonya gasped and let out a long mewl that was like fingertips gliding over my skin. I knew without looking that she'd climaxed, and—*fuck*—she sounded good, doing so.

Quentin tightened his grip in my hair and pushed into my mouth so hard I nearly gagged. The first taste of his orgasm hit the back of my throat, and he didn't let up. He emptied his load into my mouth, and I swallowed like the good boy I was.

I licked him clean, causing him to shudder, and pulled away. I swore, the instant someone touched my dick, I was going to come.

Quentin raised my head to look me in the eye. "Sonya's all sticky." His voice was gravel. "How do you handle that?"

"Let me taste her too. Let me eat her pussy until she comes again."

His grin was power. "I like it, but it's not up to me."

I looked at Sonya, who was sucking on her fingers. Her jeans had been kicked off, and she'd shoved her panties aside, leaving her glistening cunt on display.

"Let me tongue fuck you," I said.

"Okay." Her reply was breathy.

Quentin's mouth brushed my ear. "Do that, and then you can come."

"Bossy. I like it." So much.

"Damn right, you do." Quentin nudged me toward Sonya.

Not that I needed the push. I slid her panties down her legs, memorizing the feel of her silky-smooth legs against my fingertips, then kissed up the inside of her thigh.

She squirmed and sighed with each new touch, and when I dove my tongue inside her, she arched her back, grinding against my face.

I straddled one of her legs, and she bent her knee. The instant my cock brushed her skin, I had to feel more. I thrust my pelvis, writhing against her while I licked and fingered her.

Her breath came in short pants, and her juices coated my tongue and face. I wanted—needed—more. I wrote soliloquies on her pussy and murmured for her to come.

When she did, her ass came off the bed, and her cries were as tasty as any lyrics.

I shifted my body enough to move my hand to

my cock, my fingers slick, and jerked my tender shaft while her taste lingered on my tongue. When I came, it left a spray across her thigh and hip, painting her in cum.

I collapsed onto my back, my head on her other shin, as I tried to catch my breath.

"Was it like that, back in the day?" Sonya's question was soft.

"Yes, but also no."

"Oh?" Quentin asked.

Tonight would replace any stories about the past for me. Nothing I'd done back then held a candle to this. "This was so much better."

4 /
sonya

W aking up in the same bed as Jeremy and Quentin was nice. They were good friends, and made me feel safe.

Waking up with the memories of last night, of the way the two bounced off each other, was yummy.

Waking up to them, wrapped around each other, was just plain hot.

I lay next to them, floating in the lingering fun from last night. I was used to spending time with both of them, but not together.

Quentin, Megan, and I made trips like this every few months, to different cons. He had a good following as a cosplayer, and she made the most adorable plushies that she sold in Artists' Alley.

Jeremy had never joined us before. Last night, there were distinct sparks between him and Quentin. I didn't have to decipher the subtext; there was no subtlety in two men agreeing to whip their dicks out for each other.

As tempting as it was to lie here a while longer and daydream about all the ways the two of them might hook up, I should start my day. I was quiet, climbing out of bed, grabbing my phone from Quentin's stuff, and logging into my email.

There were so many new messages. I deleted the newsletter subscriptions and skipped to those from people whose names I knew. The messages were one amazing and supportive *congratulations* after another.

I opened one from another author I'd interacted with a few times, but mostly we just brushed by each other in our day-to-day online lives.

I don't know who you paid for this publicity, but we both know you didn't earn it. If you think success because you can buy people counts, you're wrong.

Whoa. What?

My gut turned in on itself, as I read the words again.

I hadn't…

I wasn't…

I started to reply, telling her she had it all wrong, then deleted it. The words sounded defensive. I should let it go or at least come back to it later, but the message taunted me.

I tried a different approach. I was sorry she saw things that way, but it wasn't—

Delete.

None of the messages I started felt right. They were apologetic or defensive or accusatory or could be twisted back on me in some way.

My phone was yanked from my hands, and I looked up to find Jeremy standing in front of me.

"Give it back." I reached for the device.

He stepped away. "I've been calling your name for the last ten minutes, and you're so wrapped up in whatever has you frustrated that you're not hearing me."

"I'm not frustrated." I had missed his getting up, though. And getting dressed. And that the shower was running in the background, and I was still sitting in a chair in my panties.

"You're scowling at your phone like it just told you that your fanfic-dot-club password is invalid, as if you haven't typed it every day since the site opened. Did you forget one of your most important rules?"

I wasn't in the mood to be lectured. "I wasn't reading reviews; it was an email. From another author. And it wasn't a big deal."

"Really?"

I sighed and told him what was in the message.

"She's wrong, and telling her that won't change her mind." His tone softened.

"I know, but…"

Holding my gaze, Jeremy crouched in front of me and grasped my hand. "I get it. Vent to me.

Every retort and justification, I'm here to listen. Do it while we're at the con. Do it all day if you need. But don't reply to her."

"Okay." The compulsion to clear my name and make her understand was strong, but Jeremy was right. Sending a response, especially when I wasn't in a good frame of mind, wouldn't do that.

"Good. Get ready and we'll head downstairs." He lightly slapped my bare thigh, and a pleasant rush surged through me. Last night's fun was lingering, but I didn't mind. Good memory.

It took Quentin longer to get ready than both Jeremy and me, but I expected that. Putting on the makeup, wig, and outfit was an event by itself. But when he was done, he looked exactly like X brought to life. Even though the series of games from Rinslet had wrapped up a few years ago, X's character was still popular.

Which I loved. X had starred in some of my very first fanfics—he was the first guy I shipped with another—and those stories were my entry into working in the gaming world.

We headed down to the con. This wasn't a huge show, but it was big enough that we'd see a variety of neat stuff over the next eight to ten hours.

After we stepped off the elevator, we were stopped every few feet so people could take pictures of and with Quentin. It took us thirty minutes to walk the short distance from the hotel lobby to the first panel.

"I knew he'd be popular, but this is way more popular than I expected," Jeremy said.

I shrugged. "You get used to it." I watched as another wave of groups posed with him and snapped photos.

"Not that I blame them." Jeremy looked Quentin over. "Pretty sure X never looked that good in the games." His tone was admiration mixed with… lust?

Maybe. Interesting. "The graphics were lower quality in the games."

"That's right, guys and gals." Quentin joined us. "Full 8K HD right here, live and in person."

"I really want there to be a sex joke in there." I followed them into the panel room, and we took seats near the back of the room.

Jeremy furrowed his brows, then smiled. "We can have him say it again later, so you can think up a better comeback."

"Nah. The moment's passed. Besides, I'm sure the two of you will give me plenty of innuendo-laden opportunities as the day goes on." And maybe some daydream fodder as well.

"Ah, the life of a romance writer." Quentin sounded wistful. "Always thinking about ways to fit more dicks in."

I let out a short laugh. "Not even ten seconds. Told you."

I was looking forward to a day full of panels, dotted with small breaks to shop and eat. It had been a while since I attended one of these as a fan. Sure, Megan was fine with me going to whatever panels I wanted, but I went to shows to help her, and I hated abandoning her.

Still, I missed having Megan here. How was our con dynamic going to change when she got married?

I shook the random question aside and enjoyed the panel. We hopped from *The History of Weapons* to *Women in Fiction* to a fanfiction panel.

I sat in on every fanfic panel I could, mostly to find new authors to read. But also, it was fun to watch the trends shift, both in series people were writing about, and the tropes and kinks as they waxed and waned.

The moderator introduced all the guests— mostly names I recognized, but with a couple brand new on the list—then paused. "And we have a special guest in the audience."

We did? I looked around, trying to find a familiar face. Was it another newcomer to the scene?

"Sonya Russel has been a part of the community for years and has spun her talent into a career."

Who?

Jeremy and Quentin were both nudging me.

Holy shit, that was me. And everyone in the room was staring at me.

Eep.

"Would you like to join us?" the moderator asked.

"I… um…" Brilliant, me. I couldn't even answer a *yes or no* question. I was a fraud as a writer.

Quentin nudged me toward the stage.

"Yeah. I'd like that," I answered as I walked to the front of the room.

The staff brought up another chair and made room for me at the table. This was surreal. I was recognizable?

My shock wore off as we dove into the panel. Answering questions with other writers was a lot of fun. Half an hour into the panel, Jeremy left, his phone pressed to his ear, but he was back a few minutes later, wearing a tiny smile.

The moderated portion of the panel ended, and people were invited to pass a mic around and ask questions.

A woman in her early twenties grabbed the mic and stood. "My question is for Sonya. Is it true that your newest book—the one that just went viral—is being made into a movie?"

I shook my head. That was so unlikely, the thought almost made me laugh. "If it is, no one's told me."

When the panel was over, I lingered a while longer, chatting with people who came to the front of the room, and even signing an eBook reader cover, for someone who had a copy of my book on their device. So. Surreal.

Jeremy and Quentin approached when we were kicked out to make room for the next panel.

"You were awesome," Quentin said.

"Judith called." So that was why Jeremy left. "Said you weren't answering your phone."

Judith was our boss and had some strict rules about people not working during their vacations. "Did you tell her why?"

"Because we confiscated your phone? I told her." Jeremy nodded. "She approved."

I struggled to think of why she'd go to so much trouble to find me. The game didn't break if something was wrong with one of my stories. Nothing at the company shut down. "Is there a problem?"

"No problem. Not for you, anyway. She says, when you make it big, she wants a chance to counteroffer before you retire from the industry forever."

I laughed but cut it off short when more pieces fit together. Judith wasn't a call-someone-to-make-a-random-joke kind of person. Especially with the effort she took to make sure I got the message. "It's a splash. Things will die down by next week, and no one will know who I am again."

"Regardless, I told her you'd hear her out if it came to that."

"Of course I will." But it wouldn't.

Quentin nodded toward the dealers' room. "Let's shop." He rarely spent much money, but he liked to see what other people were doing with cosplay.

I was a fan of the cute, unique things, and I almost always spent too much.

As we wandered through the room, Jeremy was drawn to things I'd never stopped to look at before—model kits, art, and surprise boxes.

Quentin was drawn to a leather vest that was perfect for one of his next planned costumes. He spent at least five minutes examining it and chatting up the woman who created it.

"How much?" I asked.

Quentin shook his head. "It's gorgeous, and whatever you're charging isn't enough, but I can't swing it right now. I'm sorry."

"No worries." The woman smiled. "I love what you're wearing, though."

"Just let me get it for you," I said. It was obvious he was in love with the design.

His scowl was abrupt. "No."

Okay… I didn't know how to react to that.

"Did you see this?" Jeremy tugged us both away before I could fumble for an answer.

I filled up my arms with bags of random,

adorable stuff, but I stopped short of buying the Castiel artwork on canvas. The rest of the panels were incredible, and the food was overpriced, and by the end of the day, I was pretty sure I never wanted to walk that much again.

Perfect. Day.

"I'm going to go someplace with better food options, while you guys get his makeup off," Jeremy said.

We agreed that was a good idea, and he took off. He was gone almost an hour, but that made sense, given everything. What surprised me was when he walked in with food on one arm, and two large bags.

He set the takeout down and handed one bag to each of us. "Purchases are made, Dealers' Room is closed—no take-backs."

I gasped happily when I pulled out my Castiel print. "I love it. Thank you." I gave Jeremy a hug.

He squeezed back, holding on a heartbeat longer than I expected, before letting me go.

Quentin hadn't said a word. I turned to see him staring at the leather vest from earlier, and pieces clicked into place. Jeremy must have grabbed the print for me so he'd have an excuse to buy that.

I kind of wished I'd thought of something so sneaky and sweet, but my mind was also squealing *kawaii* and figuring out where their fictional romance went next.

Quentin opened his mouth, and Jeremy pressed a finger to his lips. "Unless the next thing you say is, *Thank you, I love it*, keep it to yourself."

Quentin chomped with his teeth, and Jeremy quickly pulled back his hand.

"Thank you. I love it." Quentin ran his fingers along the details on the edges and then the stitching. "You shouldn't ha—"

"Nuh-uh. Stop talking, and try it on," Jeremy said.

Quentin grinned, stripped off his shirt, and tugged on the vest. It wasn't meant to be worn alone, but that didn't make the look any less sexy.

Jeremy licked his index finger, pressed it to Quentin's bare chest, and made a sizzling sound. "*Hot*."

They were so cute together. How had I never put them in the same room long enough to see this before? Two broken men who had sworn off love, who just needed the right relationship to make them realize the world still had some beauty in it.

I'd love to have a guy like either Jeremy or Quentin. Gorgeous, caring, intelligent, and geeky. But guys like them didn't fall for girls like me. I wasn't even *one of the guys*; I was background noise. The frumpy girl who always had her head in the clouds.

Megan would tell me not to think about myself like that, but it wasn't a cruel thought. It was the reality of the situation, and I'd had enough exes tell me something similar that I knew it was true. Hell, my mother pretty much used those exact words on more than one occasion.

But Jeremy and Quentin deserved happiness, and the sparks between them were visible. It might be a long shot, but if I could help them heal and find love with each other, I had to try.

5 /
quentin

I insisted on taking the roll-away bed the second night in the room. I had no problem sleeping on something cot-like, though I was disappointed the three of us didn't have an excuse to get naked and crawl into the same bed again.

I was used to being the first person awake in most situations, so before Sonya and Jeremy got up, I decided to make a quick run to the drug store across the street. As far as I was concerned, Valentine's Day was a scam. But Sonya was infatuated with that romantic shit, and had been writing short stories about all her favorite characters and their perfect hearts days for the last month.

The chocolates were mostly gone, but I found a peanut butter and chocolate heart, and an adorably sappy card. I grabbed something for Jeremy too, as a thanks for the vest last night. I hated taking from other people, but I appreciated the thought and the gift itself.

I felt like a bit of a schmuck, though. *Hey, thanks for the high-end leather. Here's a candy bar.*

I stepped back into the hotel room as Sonya said, "...don't think you could fit three orc dicks in that room."

"Orc dicks aren't big." Jeremy gave me a brief wave.

Sonya shook her head. "No, but the orcs attached to them are." She turned to me. "Welcome back."

"Thanks." Never a dull moment with these two, apparently. "What did I miss?"

"I woke up with a new idea for a side-quest, and we were trying to decide if there were any applicable spots for the gangbang, or if we needed to keep the sex boring." Sonya's reply was delivered with the same casual tone she used to tell me I was welcome to anything in the cupboards.

A weird blend of desire and envy flowed through me, that she was so open about sex, but that Jeremy'd been her go-to for the conversation. It made sense, given that they worked together and this was a work conversation. "I assume the one-on-one sex is the *boring* option?"

"Yeah." Sonya's tone made it sound like that was obvious. "I don't even know if we've got an appropriate designated locale for anything more than *press them against the wall and get off*."

Not a bad image, though every time I'd let a daydream stray into looking like a porno—*hey, sexy roommate I just walked in on while you were masturbating, let me help you with that*—pressing Sonya to the wall was only the beginning. "As opposed to…?"

She shrugged. "A little bondage, possibly some pain, and an extra person or two."

"Of course." I'd read her books and knew the kinds of things her mind could dream up, and she was talking about it all so casually.

What were the odds I could act out a dirty movie or two with her, without losing her friendship and my place to stay in the process? *Hell*, if she wanted someone else there, if she wanted me to make out with Jeremy first, I was good with that.

Apparently, I woke up horny. I'd take care of that later. By myself. "By the way, happy Valentine's Day." I handed her the gift. "I'm sorry it's not much."

"It's amazing. Thank you." Her smile brought the fantasies rushing back, and when she kissed me on the cheek, I wanted to push her onto the bed and take so much more than just a kiss.

Nope. I needed to stop. I handed Jeremy the candy bar I got him. "Same to you."

"Thanks."

I needed to do something to keep my mind busy.

"Do you want me to drive, so the two of you can keep brainstorming?"

"That'd be awesome." Jeremy tossed me his keys.

We checked out, loaded up the SUV, and were back on the road. Was it worth it, driving ten hours each way for one day or so of con fun? Every time, I'd answer *yes*. I loved shifting into a different character for a while, meeting all the people, and absorbing the atmosphere of the entire event.

Plus, this time, I had the incredible memory of an impromptu mutual masturbation session to add to it all. I wouldn't do any of this differently.

"Okay, remember that DLC from Distance Call Seven a few months ago?" Sonya sounded excited.

"Honestly, everything DC started to blur together for me after Three." Jeremy, not so much.

I followed the signs to take us to I-80, content to watch the road and keep half an ear on their conversation.

Sonya puffed out a sigh. "You know the one I'm talking about. Where they got that actress from the vampire show to do the voice acting."

"Oh yeah." Now Jeremy was into it. "And she was like *hold off the vampires, while I make my world famous souffle.*"

"Exactly," Sonya said. "It was ridiculous and fun and unlocked other new content. We need something like that."

There was silence for a moment, before Jeremy snapped his fingers. "Got it. What if we have a new NPC selling food, and the player has to provide *entertainment* as payment? Player's choice, and it can be as clean or as filthy as they want. Crowd judged?"

Sonya didn't answer. The pause grew long enough it was awkward, which meant she'd expected a specific type of response and hadn't gotten it. "Okay, so how about that, but—"

"Exactly different?" Jeremy laughed.

"Well, yeah. I was thinking more along the lines of the *get a celebrity to do a fun cameo* side of things."

Jeremy twisted in his seat to look back at her. "Like a special *Hide the Sausage* quest with a Hollywood hottie?"

I snorted a laugh. "I'd play that."

"Something tells me we'd get pushback from Legal." Sonya blew a loud raspberry. "Too many variables to account for, contractually, where sexual representation is involved—or something like that."

I would've assumed, if the celebrity in question said *yes*, that would be that. This was probably one reason Sonya was the boss.

"Okay, nix the celebrity idea. Especially since so many of the players are in it for the sexiness. Let's follow Jeremy's suggestion instead," Sonya said.

"So, lots of public sex and let the players vote on

what they like best? Public sex is against the game rules."

"It was your idea." Sonya sounded exasperated. "I assumed you had a work-around."

Jeremy shrugged. "I assumed you'd take it and run with it."

Their tones were light but tinged with frustration, and I was still hung up on how openly they were discussing how to make public sex a thing. Knowing that exhibitionism with a hint—or more —of submission frequently featured in Sonya's stories added to the distraction.

Sure, the conversation was about a digital world, but so much of what happened there came from their minds, and that was enough to keep me turned on. Not the most comfortable thing while I was driving. "What about, you create a sexy, dirty version of Mardi Gras for your game?" I asked. "Boobs and more, in exchange for *beads*. Let people get as filthy as they want during the festival. Fucking against the wall. Go full on bukkake in the streets and in the sheets." I was being ludicrous on purpose.

"That's brilliant. And hot." Sonya's happy reply caught me off guard, and I went from semierect to hard as iron.

"It totally is. We'll designate a public area as temporarily restricted during the festival, so we can put the appropriate *adult content* alerts in place, set up sex-laden games for prizes, and turn an entire section into orgy central for a few weeks." Jeremy spoke with so much excitement, it might as well have actually been happening.

And now I had to know. "Do you ever act these ideas out, to make sure they're plausible?"

"I guarantee you that Art does," Jeremy said.

"No. I just have a vividly dirty imagination," Sonya added.

Jesus Christ. I should stop now. Not that I could rein in my imagination—not at this point—but I didn't need to be giving either of them this glimpse into my mind. "Would you? Act them out?"

"Probably." Jeremy's response came quickly.

"With the right person?" Sonya sounded a little more hesitant. "Yes. But it would have to be someone I trusted implicitly."

Do you trust me? Because I'd be happy to consensually wreck you. "Sounds fair." At least I had some sense of restraint. Back to the game, and to reminding myself that was the point of the conversation. "Do you time something like this to release around the holiday you're spoofing? Can you pull your idea off in two weeks?"

They both laughed.

I guess I'd asked a silly question?

"We're not laughing at you," Sonya said. "But yes, we'd time it to launch with Mardi Gras, and no, you wouldn't see it until next year. All of our

49

content is coded a *minimum* of six months out, and planning starts long before that."

I used to make plans like that—the kind that extended beyond tomorrow—but when I woke up one morning, less than two years ago, to an empty bed and bank account, I learned that counting on the future was a big mistake.

6 /
jeremy

One of the great things about working for a small company was the variety of work I got to do. One of the not-so-great things was the amount. Taking a day off meant Sonya and I returned to a backlog.

I was spending the morning proofing game text, while she cycled through meetings, and I definitely had the better job. I scanned quest-response options for an upcoming event in the orc strip club and team chat scrolled by on my second monitor. Every few minutes, I glanced over to see the next wall of text from Chris, one of our developers. Fortunately, proofreading his *analysis*—see *rant*—about why Quality Assurance should've caught some bug in the code, wasn't part of my job.

I didn't need to be watching the QA channel, since Writing's work wasn't in testing right now, but their manager, Nigel, was my best friend and I liked to have his back. He got a lot of flak, both for doing his job well and for the occasional miss. He really couldn't win sometimes.

None of us was winning in this case, though. A videoblogger named *Fallyn* ran a channel called *Phallyn's Phallusies*, where she pointed out exploits and bugs in video games. The errors she found ranged from simple things, like walking through walls, to the more grievous, like earning ultimate power or unlimited gold in a matter of minutes.

She played our game *a lot*, based on how many videos she made about it. Judith wouldn't let us ban her, because Fallyn's videos were free publicity and she did some of our work for us.

The team chat flashed, and I glanced at Chris's next comment. Since it ended with *and that's why you should've caught this*, I assumed he was done.

Nigel: Since she's using exploits commonly found in games, and you're an industry veteran, you should know not to program those things in.

Chris: Because we intentionally program bugs into the game. Right.

Nigel: I assume as much as I intentionally miss them in QA.

So, this could be a *Copy* and *Paste* of half of their conversations

"If you're reading Fallyn drama instead of that game script, she'll ping you next for typos." Sonya startled me.

I grinned at the teasing in her voice, and that she was back from her meetings. "She'll ping you. I'll be fine. Come on. This is first-class drama." I gestured at the screen and glanced at Sonya.

"It's really not." She took her seat and spun to face me. "It's Real Househusbands of Gaming, and I bet it wouldn't get even a thousand hits Day One."

"No? You don't think the world wants to watch Quality Assurance argue with Development about whose fault it is that a mouse-clicking macro defeated one of their mini games?"

"I don't think the world wants to watch or read any stories about a game development company. That's some dry as toast shit right there."

I bet she could spin it into something salacious and captivating. Besides— "You and Quentin seemed to enjoy the orgy story."

"And you seemed to enjoy telling it. Did you see how good he lo—"

A sharp squeal cut through the room, and we spun to find Luna standing in the doorway. Our digital security expert and closest thing we had to a company mascot. She looked at Sonya. "I'm so sorry I'm late."

I'd rather be having this conversation than thinking about the fact that Sonya had been about to tell me how much she liked Quentin jerking off. Not a thought I needed. Not a jealousy I needed. "Late for what?" I asked.

"*O.M.G.*" Yes, Luna spoke in acronyms. She skipped the short distance to Sonya and hugged her tightly. "You're famous. *Ahhh.*"

Sonya returned the hug, her face bright pink. "I still can't believe it. I think I sold enough books to be on a bestseller list. I'm going to be refreshing the bestseller list site like crazy tomorrow to see."

"I'll help. Adrienne will help. The whole company will help." Luna's enthusiasm could be contagious, and most of us were at least work friends, but I doubted she could make that last statement happen.

"*Hell*, Fallyn will help," I said. "She's got a macro that can click a mouse a billion times a second."

Luna scoffed as she straightened up. "Already fixed on the back end. Tell them that, will you?" She nodded at my screen. "I adjusted buffer protocols, to ensure the tinier spammy actions couldn't reach our server."

I understood *spammy* and *server*. Luna was younger than most of us by about a decade, and a lot of times she acted even younger than that, but she was fucking brilliant.

"I *could* tell them, but I don't want to steal your thunder," I said.

"It's okay. No thunder. You can tell them."

Nigel and Chris were possibly the only two people

in the universe Luna didn't get along with. Or at least the only two in the company. Chris tended to be a dick, but Nigel had some different opinions about how Luna should test her work, and she didn't appreciate that.

"Sonya, celebration tomorrow night. It's for you becoming a Bestselling Author, so you have to be there. I'll tell Dustin, so he can make it epic." Luna had apparently moved on.

Sonya shook her head, but she was smiling. "Nothing's happened yet."

"But you have the sales numbers. You know you're going to make the list. The only question is, *how high?*" I'd been listening for years to Sonya talk about how amazing it would be to have an accomplishment like that. What it would take. How she wasn't the kind of writer who sold that many books. And I knew she deserved this.

"I do have the numbers."

That made it simple. "Then Luna's right. Party, tomorrow night."

After a bit more chatting, Luna left, and the QA channel got quiet when I told them she'd fixed things. Sonya and I got back to work.

I finished reading through storyline responses and moved on to a new idea we were working up. One of the things I excelled at was imitating other people's writing voice. When Sonya got stuck, she'd feed me the basics of where she wanted to go, however little or much detail she had, and I'd fill in the next bit to help kick start her ideas.

"What did you think of the weekend?" Sonya's question came out of nowhere.

I'd thought a lot about it. Not quite what she was asking, but that impromptu masturbation session had teased me off and on since it happened. I wouldn't have minded taking a page from Art's book and acting out a game scene or two in real life with Sonya. Quentin could help. "It was a lot of fun. I'd do it again."

"Quentin is great, right?"

Jealousy speared me, and I glanced at her, to see if I could get a read on why she was asking. She was staring at her computer, but not moving.

"He's all right." I measured my words. "A little rough around the edges and kind of blunt." There was no way Sonya would work out with a guy like that.

"I was thinking I'd invite him tomorrow night." There was definitely a catch in her voice this time.

Was she...? No. She wasn't thinking about making a play for him. Or hoping he'd make one for her. She'd always kept work and Quentin separate. *Hell*, she'd always kept work at arm's length, regardless. She opted not to go to the Christmas party a few months ago, because she wasn't great at company functions.

And now she was not only agreeing to let people

from work throw her a party, but wanted to invite friends as well.

"So, like, everyone? Megan and other people too?" I asked.

"Megan and I will celebrate separately." Sonya finally looked at me. "But I feel like Quentin is cut off from so many people because of his past, and you and he got along great on the trip."

I had no idea what I had to do with any of this, except that I knew a damaged guy when I saw one. Took one to know one. I didn't have a right to say who Sonya hooked up with, but she deserved better than to fall for someone who was still licking wounds from a recent divorce, the way Quentin was.

7 /
sonya

Patience was not one of my virtues, even when what I was waiting for was both a given and an unexpectedly wonderful thing. My Wednesday crawled, as I was stuck in a loop of trying not to refresh webpages, being amazed at how many books I was still selling—how many people were talking about *my* book—and pretending I was going to get any work done.

The biggest problem with this kind of distraction was it sapped my creativity.

As the clock crept toward eleven in the morning, I admitted defeat. Fortunately, I had a backup plan. I sent Luna a message asking if she was free for an early lunch meeting.

Jeremy was good for brainstorming when I had a starting point, but it was different with Luna. She radiated enthusiasm, and I was going to feed off that today, while I fumbled my way through ideas.

Luna agreed, and ten minutes later, we were settling into a table across the street from our offices, at Loading Java. This place had good coffee, the best pastries, and a great atmosphere.

Luna's best friend managed the cosplay gaming café. Violet was in a relationship with two of the richest men in the city and didn't technically need to work. But she loved the place and was a self-professed workaholic, so she put in the hours anyway.

I understood that. I'd daydreamed on multiple occasions about one of my books making it big, and me being in a position to quit my job. Retire at forty. I'd never actually expected the option to be available to me. Even now, I expected the surge of sales to die off any minute, but even if it didn't, I couldn't imagine leaving AcesPlayed. Not at this point. I loved the work and the people too much.

"Hit me with it. Where are we starting?" Luna said.

That was the problem. "I don't know." Which was the other reason I couldn't do this with Jeremy. He liked having a jumping-off point.

"Escort, fetch, make, or slaughter?"

Every quest in game fell into one of those categories at its core. My favorites were the *fetch* quests—as in *go find something or someone and bring it back*—though I tried to keep a balance available for players. If I was trying to get the brain cranking, I needed to start someplace I enjoyed. "Fetch."

"Ooh, you should have two characters who are in love, but neither knows the other cares." Luna pulled a strip off her chocolate croissant, popped it in her mouth, and chewed for a moment. "They both send the player on quests to get the perfect thing for the other, and in the end, the player gets to push them together."

Would that work with Quentin and Jeremy? The thought came out of nowhere, but it was attached to a nagging that had been in the back of my head since the trip. I doubted they were already in love, though. They were both too jaded about *happily ever after* for that to be the case. "I love it, but what if they're both trying to move on, instead?"

Luna scrunched up her nose. "And they both want a way to be grumpy, lonely bastards, but the player realizes they'd be better off together?"

"Yes." Now the ideas were sprouting. I needed to nurture them. "NPC A tells you that, if they could just rebuild their blacksmith shop, they could move on."

"And NPC B needs something to occupy their mind and time, so their heart can heal." Luna sounded excited. More than normal.

This was perfect. I wasn't sure Jeremy was looking for a way to spend his free time, but he did love to create and build, and Quentin had a life that needed rebuilding. "So the player enlists B to help retrieve supplies and to offer suggestions to A, and then the player makes sure they work together."

"And they fall in love?"

I grinned. "And they fall in love. The player may have to nudge them a little bit, but if things go well, the player unlocks another quest to help the NPCs plan their wedding."

Luna clapped. "In-game wedding outfits?"

"Complete the quest, to unlock access to in-game player marriage." I'd discussed ways to do that with the rest of the team, but none had felt right. This did. "And when we have player housing, help them build their dream home for access to that."

"I love it."

I did too. It was absolutely perfect. Plus, I could enact a version of it in real life. Step One—make sure Quentin and Jeremy were spending more time together, including doing something that helped Quentin get back on his feet. I wasn't sure what the second step was yet, but I'd figure it out. Step Three —wedding bells.

"What kinds of quests?" Figuring that out might help me draw a parallel to my real-life plan.

Luna finished her croissant. In my excitement, I'd forgotten mine. I took a big bite while I pondered the question. Not exactly a nutritious lunch, and I'd be crashing in a few hours, but not really, because I would be spending the afternoon waiting for bestseller-list news.

I couldn't focus on that—we were on a roll with this idea.

"The basics are easy," Luna said. "First the blacksmith needs a new shop, then he needs a product, then he needs customers. Maybe there's some overlap in there."

"Good point." I could work with this. It would take some more planning, but I had enough of an idea of what came next, to start nudging Jeremy and Quentin together tonight, at the party.

Yeah, patience really wasn't my thing.

Luna's phone chimed, and she glanced at the screen. "I have a vendor meeting in fifteen minutes, but I can reschedule if you need."

"No, I'm good. Thank you." I felt a lot better about everything, and enough time had passed that I might have the answer I was waiting for soon. I downed the rest of my coffee, while Luna shoved half a biscuit sandwich into her mouth in a bite that should've been impossible, and we headed back across the street.

We were waiting for the elevator when my phone rang.

"Look at us, all popular today," Luna teased.

I gave a light laugh. The number was one I didn't recognize. "Hello?"

"Hi, I'm looking for Sonya Russel."

"This is she." I stepped into an elevator car with Luna, my curiosity rising.

"This is Daisy Graves with RopeFlick. Are you the author of *Beastly Trysts*?"

My pulse was roaring so loudly in my ears, I must be hearing her wrong. Or this was a bad connection. I had the sense to not ask her to repeat herself. "I am."

"How are you today?"

Dying of a heart attack caused by waiting for too many answers. "I'm great. You?"

"Fantastic, thanks. Look, I won't waste your time. We're interested in optioning your book for television."

What in the what?

8 /
jeremy

The scream that reached me was Luna's and fell in her *excited* range—yes, she had ranges of high-pitched emotion. She and Sonya had to be back.

I was hurrying toward the noise before I finished processing the thought. I arrived in the lobby of our offices at the same time as half the crew.

"I didn't mean to disturb everyone." Luna was grinning. "Sorry. But not really. But *ahh*."

Sonya was her opposite, staring blankly, silently, at her phone.

Everyone was focused on Luna, asking what was going on, but I had a different concern. I touched Sonya's arm, and she looked up at me with wide eyes.

"Are you okay?" I asked.

She shook her head, as if trying to rattle something loose inside. "They want to buy it."

"Who does? Buy what?" That was Nigel. The noise around us had stopped, and I swore I felt a dozen gazes on us.

Sonya blinked several times and seemed to focus on me. RopeFlick wants to buy the rights to my books."

Bedlam was back, amplified by one hundred as a chorus of *no way*, *that's awesome*, and *congratulations* broke out around us.

Sonya still looked numb. "It was just a phone call. I need to see the contract. It may be bullshit. It hasn't gone anywhere yet."

"*Just a phone call.*" I tossed her words back at her, hoping she would hear how ridiculous they sounded. "How many people even get a fucking phone call?" Envy twinged inside me, but it was easy to ignore. I'd been writing screenplays for years and had yet to even get a nibble, and she was writing off someone coming to her asking for her work.

"This celebration tonight is going to be epic," Dustin said. "We need to kick things up a notch or fifty. Time to RSVP. Show of hands, who's coming?"

People raised their hands, and Dustin counted.

My younger sister would be upset if she missed this. "Plus Megan."

"Definitely." Sonya sounded like herself. "And Quentin."

Jealousy stabbed me in the gut again. I needed to deal with that.

A sharp whistle cut over the chatter, and everyone turned to stare at Dustin. He shrugged and nodded at Judith, who'd joined us. "Boss lady says, *back to work.*"

"Ask Sonya all the questions you want tonight. She doesn't have to answer them, though," Judith said.

There were some grumbles and a few more *congrats*, but the crowd dispersed quickly.

Sonya lingered, stopping Judith before she could walk away.

Interesting.

"I know movies and books are a different industry than gaming"—Sonya sounded hesitant—"but I don't suppose you could give me the name of a good contract and IP lawyer? Or a more specific starting point than an online search will?"

Judith already had her phone out. She made a few swipes at the screen. "It's in your email. Tell him I sent you. And seriously, congratulations."

"Thank you." Sonya's smile broke free of the doubt that had clouded her face, and the look was beautiful in its simplicity.

I fell into step beside her, as we headed back to the Writers' room. The AcesPlayed office space had been a satellite campus for the community college until the school took most of their courses online. Each of our teams had snagged a classroom or two and made it our own, and every room reflected the personalities of the people who worked in it.

Sonya and I had whiteboards covering most of the walls, each with a different storyline and all of its associated options laid out. We were one of the few teams with cubicles, despite there only being two of us, because when it was time to focus, we both preferred to block out the rest of the world.

"Someone wants to make a TV show. From my books," Sonya muttered as we walked into the room.

"Because you're amazing."

"I'm really not."

This was what frustrated me about her more than anything—she couldn't see the good in herself. I grabbed her wrist loosely, tugged her to a stop, and spun her to face me. "Look at me." I placed a finger under her chin and lifted her head.

She stared back, eyes wide.

"You trust me, don't you? Especially to be honest with you?" I asked.

"Yes."

"Then believe me when I say you're the best at what you do. Period. No qualifiers. I'm not saying that to make you feel better; I'm saying it because it's true."

Sonya ducked her head, but not before I saw the

corners of her mouth tug up. "I'm going to call this contact of Judith's. Cover for me?"

"Of course."

She was back a few minutes later, saying Dominic was happy to look over any contracts she received, at a reasonable rate.

An hour or two later, when Sonya got confirmation that she'd made a best seller list, coming in at number nineteen, our focus was shot for the day. Not that we'd gotten much done up to that point. We spent the time until five following one tangent of conversation after another and frequently drifting back to her saying, "I can't believe this is happening to me."

I liked seeing her this happy. She deserved this.

Her phone rang a little later, startling me. "Is that you?" I had to make sure because she usually kept her phone on *Vibrate*. The current news was extra special if she'd turned the ringer on. "It's Megan," she told me and took the call. "Hello."

"Hey, you." Megan's voice was tinny coming through the phone speaker and the cubicle wall between Sonya and me.

If she'd answered this way, she meant for me to hear. I rolled my chair to her side of the divider. "Hello," I called.

"*Hi.*" Megan's voice was bright. "So first of all, congratulations, Sonya. This. Is. *Amazing*. No surprise, of course, because you're a genius and now the world knows it, but *congratulations*."

Sonya's smile was bright enough to light the room. "Thank you."

"And… um…" Megan's cheer faded in a single breath. "I can't make it tonight. I'm so sorry. I'll take you out another night. We'll drink till we can't walk, and we'll take a cab home, and I'll give you all the celebration you deserve."

"It's okay. It was a last-minute deal." Sonya sounded sincere, and knowing her, she wasn't questioning this at all.

I wouldn't either—things happened—but I'd heard the shift in Megan's tone. A lifetime of knowing someone, and all that. "Is everything all right?" I asked.

"We're going to taste-test wedding cake tonight," Megan said.

Sounded reasonable.

"I thought you were doing that on Saturday." Now there was a hitch in Sonya's reply.

Megan sighed. "We were, but Easton can only do it tonight. He just let me know a little bit ago. I really am sorry."

Easton was Megan's fiancé. Sonya's warning look was the only thing that kept my sarcastic *what rotten timing* from slipping out. I clenched my jaw and stared back. I wanted nothing but happiness for my sister, and every time she told me something new about her husband-to-be, I questioned his motives. But Sonya insisted I was jaded and needed to keep my thoughts to myself.

Sonya turned away before I did. "Go. Eat cake," she said. "Pick a flavor you love. It's your wedding, and we'll hook up this weekend since he'll be busy."

"Sounds perfect. Congratulations again." Megan disconnected.

I rolled my chair back to my desk.

"Don't say it," Sonya warned.

"I'm not."

"You're thinking it."

"You can't stop me from thinking things."

Sonya huffed. "How can you create such brilliant love stories and still be a romance Scrooge?"

I shrugged even though she couldn't see me. "I'm just that talented." I kept my tone playful, not wanting to argue with her.

"Yes, you are." Her light laugh was a relief.

By the time five rolled around, we were beyond done working. Not everyone in the office was dealing with the same buzz, so Sonya and I headed to the brewery where Dustin had gotten us a reservation, along with a few other people from the office. The rest would join us over the next hour or so.

Sonya went to talk to Luna, Adrienne—who was in Art—and Reese. Reese didn't officially work here, though she and her band had started doing some promotional music for us on a contract basis. One of her boyfriends worked with Luna in security, though, and the other was one of our original crew —the Brandon I'd been telling orgy stories about, a couple of days ago.

Not that he'd have a problem with that.

I sought out Dustin, our Director of Marketing and the guy who made the party happen last minute.

"Thank you for this." I gestured at the room.

Dustin waved a hand. "It was a reservation and a few details."

"Still." I knew Luna had volunteered him for the job, and he slid into it without complaint, including making sure everyone but Sonya chipped in, to foot the bill tonight.

"How many people are coming?" There was a nagging dread that it would only be a few more than were already here.

"Almost everyone."

"Excellent." I grinned. It wasn't that Sonya was disliked—she got along fine with most everyone in the office—but she bailed on a lot of company sponsored social events, so my worry was that people would do the same to her. Or that they'd just not show because software developers didn't tend to be social people either.

Dustin surveyed the room. "This is a huge deal

—not even Rinslet has TV rights out there—but it's more than that. Sonya's one of us."

"I am?" Sonya's voice came from our side, and Dustin looked as surprised as I was.

"Of course you are," Dustin said.

Sonya's smile had been bright and warm every time I'd seen her today. "You realize that even if I decide to sell—which I have no idea if this is even a good offer—most options that are purchased never make it to filming, and even fewer are released to the public." She would know better than most of us; her mother was a bigwig for one of those channels that made all the romance movies.

"But none of those books are by you." I would praise her skill all day long. No one told a story, built a rich world around it and planted unique and three-dimensional characters in it, the way Sonya did.

Dustin nodded. "And none of *us* knows anyone else who's had someone want to buy the rights to their book. We're all going to celebrate this with you."

Sonya ducked her head, but not before I caught the bright red coloring her face. At the sound of someone calling her name, she turned toward the doorway.

Quentin's arrival filled me with ambivalence. I was happy to see him, but I hadn't figured out how I felt about her inviting him.

Sonya waved him over and introduced him to Dustin. Apparently, Quentin already knew Adrienne, Reese, and Luna from movie night at Sonya's.

Sonya pointed to one of the tables waiting for us. "We're sitting over there. Jeremy on the end, you next to him, and me next to you."

"You gave us assigned seating?" Quentin sounded amused.

Dustin held up a finger. "You're new here, so I'll give you the lowdown. Sonya and Jeremy usually sit with QA and the devs, instead of creative, and it's like the tech version of a boys' side and a girls' side of the room. Tonight, we're mixing it up. Mostly so we get to sit by the guest of honor."

"Brilliant master plan, right?" Adrienne grinned.

Sonya nodded. "As long as you don't seat me at a long table in front of the room, away from and above everyone else, I'm good with it."

Luna's mouth formed an *O*. "Queen of the North?"

Not quite. "Queen of the Smut. All hail," I said.

Quentin dropped to one knee at Sonya's feet, which made me raise my eyebrows. Talking about taking things to the next level.

"I should've known I was in the presence of royalty." Quentin's tone was abruptly serious. "I am but your humble servant, your highness."

As smoothly as if it were planned, Dustin

73

mimicked Quentin's gesture, chanting *Queen of the Smut. Queen of the Smut*, and half the room joined in within seconds.

Sonya was as red as her lipstick, and she pulled Quentin to his feet. "Please don't." Her voice was quiet.

Was I the tiniest bit smug that Quentin read this situation wrong? That I knew she would hate this? I stepped between her and the room and murmured in her ear, "Let's go get some air."

She nodded and let me lead her from the room.

9 /

quentin

The moment Sonya whispered *please don't*, I knew I'd fucked up.

And I was furious at myself for the mistake, and at Jeremy for being the one who got to rescue her and bring her back a short while later.

I'd apologized, but she shrugged my words off with a quiet *it's okay*. She stayed quiet as more people showed up and we sat down for dinner. But she still kept me seated between her and Jeremy.

That made me smug.

The waitresses brought the drinks back and set a blended strawberry margarita in front of Sonya.

"This isn't mine." Sonya was quiet.

I stopped the waitress from taking it away. "I ordered it for you," I told Sonya. "It's an apology."

"It's not because you're trying to get me drunk and take advantage of me?" Teasing slipped into her voice.

The hint of the Sonya I saw at home was reassuring. "Never with alcohol. Maybe with a good slashfic."

Her smile was soft and perfect.

"Hey, can we get one of those over here for Nigel?" Someone else called. There were too many faces and names for me to remember them all, and this one wasn't from Jeremy's story.

"I don't need a strawberry margarita." That was Nigel from the *Our First Orgy* story.

"What will it take to get you drunk?" Brandon asked.

Nigel shrugged casually. "Anything that doesn't have strawberry in it."

Sonya sipped her drink, her body relaxing visibly as the conversation revolved around not-her.

"What's wrong with strawberry?" Luna wanted to know. "Oh God. You don't like it, do you? Who doesn't like strawberry?" She sounded playfully offended.

A quarter of the room chimed in with *me*.

Luna pouted. "Uncultured swine. All of you. Fine. What will it take to get you drunk enough for another knife-throwing demonstration?"

Uh… what had I walked into?

"Nigel's trained," Jeremy explained to me. "And they found out at the Christmas party."

"There was knife throwing at your Christmas party?" Who were these fascinating people?

Sonya let out a small laugh. "I'm kind of sorry I missed that one." Her voice was soft, only meant for our ears, but she was unwithdrawing so that was good.

"I can throw knives without the alcohol," Nigel said.

"No, you can't. We don't have the insurance for knife-throwing. Especially with so much glass in here." That was Judith. According to Jeremy, one of the only women from those early days. She was the big boss here, and despite being one of the shorter people in the room, carried herself like the woman in charge.

I hoped whoever she was fucking appreciated the kind of power she radiated.

"Can we not talk about throwing knives?" Link was the kind of big and bulky that a lot of Marines would sell their souls for. "My manhood can't take the competition."

"Can we whip out our dicks instead?" someone else asked.

Elliot shook his head. "Still not a contest you'd win."

Ouch. Did this just turn brutal? No one looked upset.

"You weren't complaining the other night at the glory hole," Link countered.

Jeremy covered his face and peeked through his fingers. "You promised you wouldn't tell."

"So did you." Link focused on him.

If I had to step between him and Jeremy, could I take him?

"Hey." Elliot's voice was sharp. "First rule of Fuck Club?"

Obviously not *We Don't Talk About Fuck Club*.

"We write the good stuff into the game," Nigel said.

The entire room erupted in laughter, even Sonya.

This was such an odd group of people. They were obviously family, and I had an appreciation for that. A lot of their openness with their sexuality probably had to do with the work they did. Knowing that didn't stop me from thinking about the fact that half these men had fucked each other, and none of them seemed hung up on it.

Weird. Nice. But very strange.

As the meal went on, the conversation moved in waves from individual pockets to full-room discussions. Sonya relaxed more and more, and worked her way through a few more drinks as well.

I was content to down Pepsi. I preferred to keep my wits in a room of strangers, especially one this odd, regardless of how friendly they were. Besides, someone needed to drive Sonya home.

"Serious question time." Nigel leaned in as the wait staff cleared our plates away and brought dessert out. "Who are you casting as the characters in Sonya's series?"

"Paul Rudd," Adrienne said without hesitation.

Luna squealed. "I met him once. He's *so nice.*"

"Which character?" Nigel asked.

Adrienne scrunched up her face, and then grinned. "All of them."

Reese, who had insisted she was fine without dessert, stole a forkful of Sonya's chocolate cake. "I can see that."

"Nope." Sonya playfully swatted her hand away when Reese came back for a second bite. "Not every role. I need Gary Oldman in there too."

"As who?" I asked.

"It doesn't matter." Sonya shook her head. "He's so good, he's so good, he could be playing Paul Rudd playing every character, and you'd never know it wasn't a dozen different actors on the screen."

I didn't dare argue with such intensely flawed logic, but I did laugh.

By the end of the night, Sonya's cheeks were pink from the liquor, not embarrassment, and she was spitting out thoughts one after another. "So picture this—vampires in space plus video gam— *Oh.*" She looked at me. "We should go home."

"Probably a good idea," I said.

She looped her arm through Jeremy's. "And bring him."

79

"We should drop him off at home." I hadn't planned on another passenger, but he'd had as much to drink as Sonya.

"No." Sonya shook her head so hard, she lost her balance. "Jeremy's coming home with us."

I steadied her. "Why?" The vampires needed someone to game with?

She smooshed a finger to her lips. "It's a *secret*."

"I'm good at keeping secrets," Jeremy said.

They were both kind of adorable right now, and the booze had knocked twenty years off their personalities. "All right. Quentin's Cab now in service. Everyone aboard."

Sonya snickered. "Litter… Aloo…"

"Alliteration." Jeremy laughed.

Fucking writers. They were still cute, though. Especially Sonya's half-scowl at not finding the words she wanted.

We climbed into my car and headed toward home.

"So, these vampires…" Jeremy twisted in his seat to look at Sonya. "Are they playing the games or are they trapped in the games?"

"Both. Definitely both. Like, most of them are just playing, but there's someone trapped in the game who's probably a vampire, because only vampires play the game, but she might also be Alice."

I frowned. "From *Resident Evil*?"

"From *Alice in Wonderland*." Sonya paused. "But *ooh* both! Yes. And they could fight vampire zombies and eat cakes and drink tea and blow up spaceships."

I was starting to understand the rules here—as in, there weren't many. "If they're trapped in the game, how do they know it's not their ship they're blowing up?"

"Maybe it is." Sonya sounded excited. "And that's part of the drama."

We were still discussing the logistics of vampires in space in video games when we got home. Sonya stumbled taking off her shoes, and again stepping into the living room that was two stairs lower than the entryway. She was going to hate the hangover in the morning.

"Stay right there." I hurried into the kitchen and returned quickly with water for both her and Jeremy. "Drink this."

Sonya giggled. "Yes sir."

Fuck, I liked the way she said that.

"So what's this secret?" Jeremy asked.

Sonya set her half-empty glass on the coffee table, having enough presence of mind to use a coaster even when she was drunk. "Okay, okay, okay. So listen to this, 'cuz it's brilliant."

"We're listening." And I was very curious.

"I think that the two of you"—she jabbed us

each lightly in the arm—"would be super cute together."

I looked Jeremy over. He was certainly attractive, and we'd make sexy as fuck porn together, but knowing Sonya, that wasn't what she meant.

"Why?" I asked at the same time Jeremy did.

Sonya huffed and rolled her eyes. "You're both smart. And single. And you get along. Sparks. *Boom.*" She made an explosion gesture with her hands.

"We're both single on purpose." Jeremy said what I was thinking.

Sonya scowled. "You have to at least give it a try. A kiss. Something."

"Most relationships don't *start* with a ki—"

Jeremy crushed his mouth to mine, cutting me off. A rainbow of reactions lit through me, from surprise to desire. Even drunk and sloppy, his kiss seared my senses.

But I wasn't letting him control this situation. I shifted my weight, controlling and deepening the kiss while I nudged him back toward the couch.

He raked his fingers down my chest, shifted his weight, and ground his hip into my growing erection. Snippets of his orgy story teased me, mingling with images of what he looked like, jerking off. What Sonya looked like.

And she was watching us. She had to be enjoying this. Her groan confirmed that.

Now I was harder. There were probably a billion reasons not to do this, but all I could think about were the reasons to keep going.

Jeremy stumbled, breaking the kiss and landing on the couch on his ass. The room seemed to pause, and then he and Sonya started giggling.

Giggles became loud laughs and gasps for air.

There was my Number One reason to stop— they were both drunk.

"Both of you, to bed." I pointed Sonya toward her room and Jeremy toward the guest room.

Sonya grabbed our hands and tugged. "After that? You're coming with me."

We most certainly were not.

I let her lead the way because it would be easier to get her to her room.

She fell into bed, pulling on our arms. "Don't go." Her tone had shifted to sad. "I promise I'll behave. I just want company."

This was such a bad idea. "Okay." I climbed into bed next to her, unable to ignore the way my pulse roared when she pressed into my side and laid her head on my chest. My jealousy roared louder when Jeremy settled on her other side.

Sonya kissed my shoulder, the heat of her lips searing through my shirt. "Thank you." She sounded drowsy.

I lay there wide awake long after the two of them fell asleep, sorting my thoughts into nice, neat columns and making sure any feelings I had about tonight were stashed away before morning.

Hours later, I had to admit that wasn't happening, and I only saw one other solution.

Fuck it. Once Jeremy and Sonya were sober, I was going to see if either or both were interested in making our relationship physical.

10 /
sonya

Last night was one of the best nights of my life. And yet, I felt like I'd missed out on something important. I remembered all of it—I hadn't been *that* drunk—and I felt it all, too. I'd wanted Quentin and Jeremy to keep going.

At the same time, I'd wanted one of them to kiss me. That was selfish and stupid. I wasn't the girl who got the guy; I was the girl who wrote about the guy getting the guy. And now I was in bed between those guys, one pressed into my back and the other one acting as an uncomfortable but soothing pillow.

I scooted off Quentin's arm and opened my eyes.

He was staring back, dark lashes framing a thoughtful gaze. "Morning."

I started to open my mouth, and more reality sank in at the coated feeling on my tongue. I smiled instead.

"How are you feeling?" he asked.

I covered my mouth, hoping to shield him from what I assumed was toxic morning breath. "Like a horde of zombie strawberries died on my tongue."

His chuckle mingled with Jeremy's, sending a pleasant shiver down my spine.

"You think your mouth zombies are related to my mouth fungus?" Jeremy asked.

Quentin winced. "I was going to say something, but I'm pretty sure the two of you have ruined the moment."

"What? No." I wouldn't let him drop a line like that and not explain. "Say it."

Quentin shook his head and booped me softly on the noise. "Go brush away the zombie strawberries, so you're not hung up on them. I'll make coffee." He extracted himself from us and walked out of the room.

Nice view. Was Jeremy appreciating that as much as I was?

I flopped back with a sigh, colliding with Jeremy, who rested his head against the back of mine. "Is this awkward? That we're making a habit of falling asleep in the same bed?" he asked.

"Is twice a habit?"

"More of one than once."

I didn't want it to be awkward. That was the last thing I wanted. "How many overnighters have we pulled over the years?"

"More than I care to admit."

"See? It's fine." I wasn't sure my logic worked, but I was going to pretend it did. "Do you want mouthwash?"

"Or something." Jeremy made a lip-smacking sound near my ear.

A glance at the clock said I was up earlier than normal, which meant I could drag my feet getting ready for work. That was good. I wanted time to enjoy the company.

A short while and a bit of mouthwash later, I felt like we'd killed off most of the lingering liquor taste from last night.

Jeremy and I found Quentin in the kitchen, sipping from one mug, with two more on the table. His hair was damp, and he was in fresh clothes. He'd managed to shower and make coffee while we were still getting out of bed. He must be part wizard.

I took a long swallow of coffee and cringed.

"Doesn't mix well with mint, does it?" Quentin sounded amused.

I set the mug down. "What were you going to say in the bedroom?" If I didn't find out now, it would bother me all day.

He looked past me toward Jeremy, then shook his head. "Nothing."

"Nope. That won't fly here." I was way too

curious and anxiety ridden to brush off a statement like, *I was going to say something sweet, but…*

Quentin looked at Jeremy again before settling a hand on my cheek and meeting my gaze. "If you hadn't been drunk last night, things would've gone differently."

My brain stalled, refusing to interpret his words or his look or his touch. "With Jeremy?"

"With you." Quentin dragged a thumb over my bottom lip. "I'm not looking for romance, and I know that's one of your things, but—*fuck*—I want a taste of the body that goes with that brilliant mind. And if he's there as well, that's fine."

My book going viral. The TV offer. My gorgeous roommate, telling me he wanted… to fuck me?

I couldn't process this kind of world. This didn't happen to real people. It didn't happen to fictional ones. Life wasn't this kind unless it intended to stick the knife in and break it off at the hilt. "Is this an elaborate joke? A dream I'm not going to wake up from?"

"You wanted to know what I was going to say in bed. This is it." Quentin's voice was low and deep, rumbling over and through me. He slid his hand to the back of my neck and claimed my mouth.

The hunger in his kiss made me whimper, and my world tilted off its axis. I didn't… I couldn't…

What? I gripped his shirt in my fists, needing something to cling to, to keep my mental footing.

That didn't help. The way his tongue danced with mine and his fingers dug into my skin flooded me with an all-consuming need.

I'd never had a dream like this before. And he was kissing the wrong person. I almost hated the thought, but he belonged with Jeremy.

Quentin glided his free hand down my side. It brushed the edge of my breast, slid lower, and rested on my hip, his thumb teasing under my waistband. He twisted us both, until my back met the fridge. My body had no choice but to mold to his hard, chiseled form.

I'd do anything he asked, and not think twice about it.

When he broke the kiss, I gasped. The world that rushed back in, but I couldn't look away from him.

Jeremy's barking laugh shattered the mood. "*Wow.* No, really. He was kissing me last night, and now he's sticking his tongue down your throat? Who will you find him kissing tomorrow?"

"*You* kissed *me* last night," Quentin countered. "At her prompting. And you're the one with stories about how many of your co-workers you've fucked at the same time—not that I'm complaining. Are you really throwing shade? Besides, the offer is open to both of you."

That made so much more sense than Quentin wanting me, and everyone knew the right *no strings attached* agreements frequently led to the sweetest long-term relationships. If I got to participate and nudge them together at the same time... That was a hard offer to walk away from.

"I've always wondered what two guys at once would be like." I looked at Jeremy. "And you can't tell me *co-workers with benefits* isn't a thing."

"It was a good kiss last night. And watching you two together..." Jeremy closed the distance between us, cupped my cheek without pushing Quentin out of the way, kissed me.

The spark at his light touch blazed when he knotted his fingers in my hair and shifted my body toward him. The way he nipped at my bottom lip then licked away the sting was more playful than Quentin's kiss, but just as intense. Just as breath stealing.

Jeremy pulled his lips from mine and searched my face. "You have no idea how long I've wanted to do that."

"He said, as if they'd known each other for an eternity." I didn't typically narrate my own life unless I ran out of anything else to say. Apparently, these men made me thought-tied.

"When's your first meeting, Sonya?" Jeremy asked.

"Nine thirty."

He tugged me away from the fridge. "Shame we don't have more time. We could have you for breakfast."

"Ooh, I like the way you think." Quentin spun me to face him and teased a finger along the inside of my waistband.

Jeremy brushed my hair off my neck and trailed his lips along my skin, up to my ear. "Strip you down. Drizzle honey all over you and lick you clean. Watch Quentin fuck you and I can have cream pie for dessert…"

Or cook an egg on my flaming hot skin. *Oh Goddess.* Did I know Jeremy could harness the power of filthy language? Of course, it was what we did. But this new trend of his using it on me?

Few things were hotter.

"I assume we can skip a lot, since you two are in a hurry." Quentin shoved my shirt up, the friction teasing my skin.

Drawn-out foreplay had its place, but the way Quentin yanked my bra down and captured a nipple in his mouth made me feel like I was his lifeline. He sucked and bit the skin, sending fissures of delight through me.

"I still remember how good your pussy tastes." Jeremy undid my jeans and teased his hands under my panties. "I guess I have to be satisfied with memories of you grinding against my face. For now."

Quentin worked his hips, pressing his erection into my thigh as he sucked on my nipples. He dug his fingers into my ass cheeks, holding me tight while Jeremy stroked my clit. The attention from so many directions at once built inside, pushing me closer and closer.

My breath escaped in short gasps as Quentin sucked and Jeremy fingered me. I whimpered when I came, riding the wave until the pleasure ebbed.

Jeremy pulled his touch away, but I still felt him behind me.

Quentin hovered his mouth over mine, then hesitated.

"That's disappointing," he murmured.

My heart seized. "What is?"

"Condoms are in the bedroom, and I really want to fuck you *now*."

I let out a barking laugh of relief and rested my palms on his chest. "Are you clean?"

"Yes."

I was on birth control, and this was too good to pause for even a second. "Then I don't care. Fuck me. Come inside me. Just don't stop."

"You say the sexiest things." Quentin's chuckle was strained. He spun me away from him, and yanked my bottoms down to my knees, restricting my movement. He glided his fingers along my slit to penetrate me. "*Fuck*, he made you wet." He pumped lightly, teasing me.

I was working on a witty-but sexy comeback when Quentin slid out of me. Before I could catch up, he gripped my hips tight, and slammed his cock into me. A gasp tore from my throat instead of words.

Quentin pressed me forward, his hands between my shoulder blades, until I was bent at the waist, supporting myself with my hands on a stool. When he wrapped my hair around his hand and yanked, my head jerked back. I groaned in surprise and delight.

"You look delicious." Jeremy stepped in front of me. "Trapped. Flushed." He dragged his thumb along my bottom lip and pressed it into my mouth. I licked along the pad, watching him with wide-eyed innocence and smirking with satisfaction when his eyelids fluttered.

I was intently aware of Quentin moving slowly in me, keeping my head pulled back with his grip. Being trapped like this, between the two of them, was enough to make me slick all over again.

"The most amazing thoughts come out of your mouth." Jeremy popped his thumb out, and lifted my chin. "And I've fantasized so many times about fucking it."

He'd fantasized... about me? I licked my lips and held his gaze.

Jeremy slid down his zipper, worked his cock free, and pressed the head to my lips. I opened my mouth to let him in. When I teased my tongue along his skin, his grunt was intoxicating.

With me pinned between them, Quentin and Jeremy hit a steady rhythm. Jeremy slipped out of my mouth occasionally, but always found his way back, while Quentin slammed deep inside me, fast and hard.

I slid into the attention of being trapped. Of being stuffed in the most literal and wonderful way. When Jeremy struck the back of my throat too hard, I had to swallow back a gag, but it didn't matter. I was lost in the moment.

Quentin let go of my hair and sought out my clit. When he pressed into the swollen nub, it was both too much and not enough. I tried to thrust into his hand. There was no way. I was stuck whimpering for more.

I loved every bit of it.

Quentin circled my clit, and another orgasm built inside me. My world shattered in ecstasy. I didn't know where Jeremy stopped and Quentin started. All I knew was how incredible this felt.

When Jeremy grunted, and a salty-warm spurt filled my mouth, it added to the moment. I licked hungrily.

Quentin moved both hands to my hips, gripping so tightly he was going to leave marks. I swore I felt him spill inside me.

I floated away on the feeling of a drawn-out

climax, floating down again as the intensity in the room faded, but didn't vanish.

I was remembering this moment forever, in case I never got another like it again.

Showers were normally my morning brainstorming time, when I thought through any plot issues I was having, in preparation for the workday. This morning, I couldn't stop thinking about what just happened.

Jeremy and Quentin really were perfect together. They seemed to read each other's moves and desires. And *Goddess*, the way they made my body react... As much as I wanted to, I couldn't get used to being a part of things, but I'd enjoy the sex while I was involved, and this arrangement would make my plan to nudge them together so much easier.

Next steps were figuring out how to get Quentin into a new workshop and how to keep him from protesting the cost, and how to make sure Jeremy was at the helm of the entire thing.

I'd figured out interactions on fifty-seven overlapping side-quests and storylines, to determine all of the possible outcomes and permeations of doing them in any order. I could puzzle through this simple thing. At the same time, I could appreciate how good it felt to be a part of it, because—*wow*—this morning was a lot of fun. My skin was buzzing from the experience.

When I emerged from the bathroom, Jeremy was waiting in the kitchen with Quentin. Neither of them was speaking. Jeremy was about the same height as Quentin but not as broad in the shoulders, so the borrowed clothes made him look thinner than he really was.

Just like the cute, skinny guy in any great anime pairing.

"Did I interrupt?" As in, had I walked into the middle of some light flirting that neither of them wanted me to see?

Jeremy shook his head. "Nope. Just sipping the coffee and basking in post-coital bliss."

Comfortable silence wasn't quite as good as flirting, but it was better than uncomfortable silence.

While Quentin drove us to work, I scanned my email. The initial offer from RopeFlick was waiting in my inbox. This was really happening. *Holy shit.* I forwarded everything to Dominic.

Quentin stopped his car between Jeremy's and mine in the restaurant parking lot. "We're all good? You won't come home and be awkward tonight?" he asked.

"I'm good. I'm really fucking good," Jeremy said.

I nodded. "Ditto that."

It was a short drive to the office, and I arrived at the same time as Jeremy. There wasn't any chance for chatting, though. "I have to be in that nine-thirty." I watched seconds tick by, as we rode the elevator up to our floor.

"I'll cover for you," Jeremy said.

We went our separate ways when we reached the offices.

I stepped into the conference room at nine thirty-two, just in time for every other member of management to stare at me as I took my seat.

"Sorry I'm late," I said softly. How long until everyone in the office knew I'd arrived at the same time as Jeremy, and started speculating?

Not that it mattered. No one here cared who fucked whom, as long as it was consensual and everyone involved was having fun.

"Everyone's allowed one tardy in their career. Especially when they were celebrating amazing news the day before by getting very drunk." Judith barely looked up from her laptop. "As long as we can get started now."

"Definitely. Yes." I set up my machine.

Judith ran through the basics of any Thursday-morning management meeting. "Upcoming changes to the employee handbook—you're all responsible for making sure your teams acknowledge this change."

Her tone caught my attention, but not as much

as the words did. We rarely changed company policies, and when we did, the changes tended to be little wording things that clarified what already existed.

"We're adding a *no fraternization* section." Before Judith finished speaking, the room erupted in a chorus of, *What? No.*

I kept my protest to myself, but my mental response was the same.

Judith sighed. "I've held this off as long as I can, but we all knew this was coming. As we hire more people who didn't come from our background, we have to be more careful about the legal nature of our company. It's simple—existing relationships are exempt, of course, but no dating anyone you work with—"

"So if we're already fucking someone?" Elliot asked.

Judith stared at him. "Are you?"

"No."

Not technically. Most of the office knew that Elliot and Link were spending time outside of work in-game screwing an anonymous person's avatar, and each other's.

Judith rolled her eyes. "Romantic relationships. You all know what it means, and this is *not* an invitation to look for loopholes. I trust you all to be adults and keep in mind that the in-game chat stores all conversations for legal purposes."

"I realize. I wrote the logging," Elliot said.

"This goes into effect next month. Get the fucking out of the way now, and you need to make sure all of your teams understand. Clear?" Judith asked.

Everyone including me nodded our agreement.

So much for no-strings fun with Jeremy. But there was no rule against his being with Quentin. Pretty sure that wasn't even a loophole. Still, there was a hum of longing inside for more of what I'd had this morning. Best I cut things off now, so it didn't hurt to do so later.

We worked through the rest of the agenda, and I tried to keep my focus on the meeting. Every time I managed to shove aside an avalanche of thoughts, my phone would buzz.

By the time I got out of the meeting, I was itching to talk to Jeremy, to listen to messages, to see if Dominic had replied to my email this morning…

To do *something* other than sit in a meeting.

When we finally wrapped up, *School's Out* played in my head. I scanned the text transcripts of my voicemails as I walked back to my desk.

This is Ada with MAXHobo. I'd like to discuss Beastly Tryst with you. Give me a call?

Hi, Sonya. I'm Michael with Moonz I'm hoping you can make room in your schedule to chat today.

I leaned against a nearby wall for support while my head spun with thoughts that refused to become words. Whose life was I living? I turned my attention to the last message.

Sonya, it's your mom. I saw all the attention your little book has been getting. Congratulations, hon. You and I both know this kind of popularity, especially for the kind of things you write, is a bright flash of a trend, and whatever comes along tomorrow will outshine it. But we want to work with you. With a few adjustments, you can turn now *into* long term *and a long stream of movies through us.*

Here was reality. I was famous because the world had discovered something fandom circles had known for years—that kinky threesomes could be fun too—and that fascination wouldn't last.

How had I started to convince myself otherwise?

11 /
jeremy

When Sonya got back, her weak *hey* yanked my attention from my work.

I rolled my chair to her desk in an instant. "What's wrong?"

"Nothing."

Uh-huh. "Something bad happen?"

She looked up, but it was more through me than at me. "New anti-fraternization rule for the company. Goes into effect next month."

"Oh. That sucks." A lot. This morning was fun, and I was looking forward to doing more that ran in a similar vein. "That only applies to dating, right?"

"You know better than that." She definitely sounded off.

Next month meant we still had almost two weeks to have fun. "What's really going on?"

Sonya finally smiled, but it didn't reach her eyes.

"Three more companies are interested in rights to my books."

"That's great."

"Including my mom's." Her tone was even and devoid of emotion.

"Oh. *Wow.*" I didn't know much about her past with her mother. They rarely spoke, but every conversation they'd had since I met Sonya left her defeated and withdrawn. "How'd that go?"

"I haven't talked to her yet. She called while I was in the meeting."

I was all about family. The people in this company were family. My sisters were family. But the things that controlling parents could do to a person...

Sonya's relationship with her mother was a slow, brutal deconstruction, and Sonya shrank into herself after every conversation they had. I hated seeing it.

She blinked a few times and shook her head. "Anyway. I should call them back, and you should get back to work."

"You got it, boss."

I tried not to eavesdrop too much, but she stayed in the office while she called people back. The first two calls were brief, and Sonya sounded pleasant through both.

The instant Sonya got her mother on the line, her

tone shifted to dejected and submissive. The longer the call went on, the more defensive Sonya grew, hesitating with her answers and stammering when she finally got each one out. I caught phrases like *but that's central to the story* and *if you take that out, the plot changes significantly.*

"No, you have a good point," Sonya sounded defeated. "Send it over, and I'll forward it to my attorney… Not until he's looked at it."

At least she was staying firm on that.

She disconnected, and the clacking of her fingers on the keyboard filled the abrupt silence in the room.

Sonya was quiet most of the time, the kind of person who raised her hand in a meeting if she had something to say, but she was intelligent and the best at what she did. She took a stand when she needed to, and she got shit done.

Every time she talked to her mother, she withdrew into her shell after. How long depended on how intense the conversation was.

"You're not going to let anyone change your books, are you?" I tried to leave the question generic.

"Only enough to make them fit the format. Books don't translate to screen, word for word."

Good evasion. "That's fair. I'll phrase it differently—are you going to retain creative rights?"

"I don't think I have that kind of pull. Do you

know how rare it is for a creator to retain that kind of input once they sell?"

And how many times had her mother driven that and other points home to reinforce her opinion of Sonya's work—her very *wrong* opinion?

"You have four offers on the table. You have that kind of pull." Inspiration struck. "What if you had a proposal of the things you'd like to see happen before you sat down at any negotiating table? That way, you're not tossing out a generic *this has to be my way* and if they suggest things you're not happy with, you've got the answers on hand."

"That does sound helpful." Sonya's silence stretched on for a second and then more. Was she done talking, or was she thinking? "*Oh*. You could help me with that. Would you?"

"I'd love to." Was I daydreaming just a little of a writer credit on her TV show or movie? Yes. I wouldn't deny that. But this was more about making sure she didn't get fucked in all the wrong ways.

"You're the best. Thank you." She sounded better than she had since she got back from her morning meeting.

Silence settled into the Writers' room again, but this time it felt natural. This was the atmosphere we usually worked in.

"So I have this idea for a new quest." Sonya's statement came out of nowhere.

I liked ideas. Especially if they were tied into the

one we had on our trip. "An add-on to the not-Mardi-Gras stuff?" Something sexy and possibly filthy? Talking dirty had been a part of our job for years, but after our road trip, after this morning... I wanted even more than normal to hear Sonya's ideas about sex in game.

"No. Something totally different," she said.

Weird. "We don't have something *totally different* on the schedule." Not that I had a problem talking about any idea, but ignoring deadlines wasn't like her.

"We can fit something in."

That's what she said. Though I was surprised to hear her say that. "That's not how this works. You're the one who reminds me all the time that we don't just *fit things in.*"

"I'm the boss, and I say we can."

What? She'd *never* pulled that card before, and the slice of her tone put me on edge. "Fine, *boss.* What are we fitting in?" I didn't mean for the question to come out harshly.

"Forget it. You're right. It's a stupid idea, anyway."

What the actual fuck? Was this because of the conversation with her mother? Was it something else? Whatever was going on with Sonya, it wasn't normal. I rolled my chair to her cubicle so I could look her in the eye for this conversation. "What are you doing?"

"Working. On story ideas. Some of which are apparently super bad." She stared at her screen, but her hands were tucked into her lap as she fiddled with her fingers.

My frustration surged. I didn't care for the self-effacing tone, and while I was used to Sonya doubting herself, this was different. "*Stop.*" I tried to find that line between forceful and kind, and I wasn't sure I managed. "You haven't told me the idea, and we don't have bad ideas, remember? We have ideas that start out amazing, and ideas that become amazing once we polish them." The words came from her, not me. It was a philosophy she brought to the team when she started at Rinslet. "If you feel we can fit this in the writing schedule, I trust you."

"But Dev will push back. And Art. And Music."

"Probably. That doesn't mean we can't flesh the idea out now and slot it in for later."

She finally looked at me, her expression clear and her smile almost genuine. "It really is okay. I was thinking it might be fun to do a quest where the player has to help an NPC blacksmith rebuild his shop."

"And the reward is a huge weapon upgrade?" I loved the idea.

She sucked in a sharp breath through her teeth. "I was thinking it would unlock player marriage and housing."

Wow, I was really missing something. "Okay…?"

"I'm not explaining this well."

"Help me understand it. Those are two quests we have on the schedule. If this is the best way to get there, let's do it."

She shook her head. "I need to think it through more first, and this whole TV rights-slash-book fame thing is screwing with my head."

"I'm here when you're ready." And a bit frustrated and perplexed in the meantime.

I suspected what was really screwing with her head was the phone call with her mother, but the entire conversation I just had with Sonya was off, and I was missing something bigger than what was on the surface.

12 /
quentin

I didn't need to listen to the voicemail again. I'd heard it three times, and it didn't contain any useful information.

So why was I standing in the middle of the kitchen, staring at my phone like it could offer me any answers for why my ex-husband had called out of the blue and said, *I need to talk to you. Please. Call me back.*

I should delete the message. Or use the phone number to see if it led to an address—not for me, but for a lawyer to send a letter, trying to collect the hundreds of thousands of dollars that Mick had stolen from me. Not that I could afford a lawyer for anything.

"Is the sex a sticking point?" Jeremy's voice drifted toward me from the living room.

He arrived before ten this morning, and he and Sonya had been working a rough script for her book for the last hour or so. They were talking about the steamier parts of her story, and it sounded like my kind of distraction. Especially since I had specific opinions about those.

"I'd rather those things didn't get cut, but if they have to…" Sonya sounded reluctant.

I strode into the room. "It's central to the heroine's arc. If you tame or take out the sex, it diminishes the way she heals and her reconciliation."

Jeremy pointed at me. "What he said."

"My mom said the shock value of the sex won't appeal to the market once the thrill dies down." Sonya sank into the couch and crossed her arms. "That people like it now because a lot of them never read it before, but once it becomes old news, they'll realize it's over the top and"—she frowned—"*repulsive*." Her voice grew quiet.

Jeremy's growl matched the one in my head. "Her words?" he asked.

Sonya shrugged.

"Your mother produces movies that all follow the same seven beats and imply that no one ever has sex and that people don't even kiss until they're in love." I'd spent a lot of time listening to Sonya discuss story structure, and it fascinated me. "To each their own, honestly." I'd been sucked into my fair share of holiday romances. "But people like your books because they're good books that let them admit that thinking dirty thoughts doesn't make them deviants."

Sonya's scowl deepened. "She's got a lot of experience."

This wasn't a path I wanted to go down. "You and Jeremy are the experts when it comes to this book stuff. You know your story better than anyone, and you know what would do it justice."

"What would it take to get you welding again?" Sonya's question came out of nowhere, smacked me in the chest, and reminded me of the voicemail I needed to delete.

"Clients who trust me. My contractor license restored."

"What if you had a client who trusted you and who wasn't worried about your license because what she wanted wasn't an *I need a license* kind of thing, and she knew you weren't the reason you lost it anyway?"

Sonya's use of pronouns instead of her name didn't fool me, and I wasn't interested in her pity or charity. "Who?"

"Megan."

Jeremy looked as surprised as I was.

"For what?" I asked.

"Okay, so it's for her, but really I'd be the one hiring you, but it's for her." Sonya said quickly.

Yup. There it was.

"It's a legitimate job, I swear to you." Sonya was still going. "She found this perfect arbor for her wedding, but it's *way* expensive. Like, it would cost her as much as the rest of the wedding. I'd love to get one for her as an early gift, and also 'cause—you know—Maid of Honor, but there has to be an alternative."

Jeremy stared blankly at her for a moment. "Fuck me."

"Later, if you want." My retort slipped out without thought.

Sonya's soft smile was worth it.

"Is this what the other day was about?" Jeremy asked.

Sonya's expression shifted in an instant. "No. I told you, I need more time for that."

"But you were asking about—"

"Nothing." Sonya cut him off. "Look. Megan sent me pictures." She scrolled through her phone and showed me the image.

The frame was wrought iron that looked like woven vines, like plants frozen in time. It had an elegant, elven feel, like something straight out of a fantasy movie.

"That's a really cool idea." I had to admit.

"Could you do something like that?" Sonya asked.

I took the phone from her to get a closer look at the screen and examined the different angles. I'd played with sculpting a bit, for fun. "Maybe." It looked like an amazing challenge. "Probably."

"This is exactly what the other day was about." Jeremy was really hung up on that. "You didn't want an in-game quest; you wanted help figuring out…" He snapped his jaw shut.

Sonya winced.

The idea looked like fun, but I didn't have the equipment, and I definitely wasn't interested in their schemes or their pity. "I'll think about it." I wanted to go back to the other subject before I lost my cool over this contrived conversation. "Are you really considering ditching the sex part of your book?"

"I don't want to." Sonya puffed out her cheeks, and they deflated when she sighed. "You're right that it's at the core of her arc."

"You know which part has always been one of my favorites?" Thinking about it sent heat racing through me and was a welcome distraction. "Second book, when they finally reach that middle ground of understanding. When the sex is rough but the emotional pain is starting to bleed away."

"One of my favorite parts too," Jeremy agreed.

Fuck. I wouldn't mind reenacting it now—an actual nooner. I'd love if playing out the scene from her book didn't have any of the same *heart and soul ripped out* elements, but at least in real life, we hadn't done that to each other. Our scars came from other people, like the man whose message was on my phone, taunting me.

Nope. Wasn't thinking about that. I was picturing bringing that intense, rough, sexy scene in her book to life. "You have to keep that."

"What did you like best about it?" Sonya watched me, bottom lip caught between her teeth.

I stalled. Words weren't my thing, even though I knew what I wanted to say.

"Your heroine has been disappointed so many times in her life, been beaten down, that she expects it." Jeremy had the perfect words for what I was thinking. "But her guys are there for her now, helping her through the trauma from her past. She trusts them enough that she's given them the power to do what they want to her."

As he talked, I couldn't help but draw a thumb along Sonya's bottom lip, recreating the same mood we were discussing from the book. A quiet power that enveloped the characters that I wanted wrapped around us.

Sonya gasped at the light touch and parted her lips. "And?" Her question was breathy.

"She's been with them long enough she trusts them with both the pleasure and the pain," Jeremy said. "And both are part of her healing."

I pressed two fingers into her mouth and she drew them in, sucking hungrily. Need scorched me from the inside out when her eyelids fluttered.

Jeremy watched us with an intense gaze. "She's learned that she has the ultimate control." His voice was husky. "She can stop them at any time." He shoved her shirt up, exposing her. "And she trusts them to listen."

Fuck he was good.

He hovered his mouth near her ear. "Which is exactly why she can let them keep going."

I dropped my hand to the button on her jeans. "Will you do that? Give me—us—permission to do whatever we want to you?" I undid the clothing.

"Yes." Sonya's voice was sweet and yielding. "You have my permission to use me however you want."

Perfect. In a single motion, I lifted her to bend her over my knee, and yanked her jeans down enough to expose her ass. Her squeal of surprise took me from half-erect to full-on rebar.

I slipped my fingers along the inside leg of her panties, then yanked up, wedging the cotton between her butt cheeks. Working the fabric, I teased and made sure it rubbed along her slit until she was squirming and sighing.

When I slapped one cheek, she groaned.

So delicious. Especially with Jeremy setting back on the couch and stroking the outline of a hard-on through his trousers.

I spanked her again and again, alternating cheeks until her ass was almost glowing read and she was half-panting, half-whimpering. Jeremy's breathing was almost as shallow as Sonya's, and I was hard enough to fuck a hole through a wood board.

If I were carrying my knife, I'd be tempted to slide the flat side of the cold steel along her skin and cut her panties off. I settled for something gentler and less destructive, sliding the lingerie down her legs and stripping her bare from the waist down. I smoothed my hand along the curve of her behind, being gentle with her tender skin, and slipped two fingers inside her.

"I bet her pussy is dripping wet." Jeremy said in a growl.

I did like the way he had with words, especially the crude ones. "Like a faucet."

"*God* I like watching you fuck two together. Your fingers inside her. Your cock…"

I was pretty fond of it as well. I teased Sonya, pumping in and out in a slow rhythm, until she was clenching and grinding against my hand. Her sigh when I withdrew was intoxicating.

I pressed my fingers to Jeremy's lips this time and he sucked me clean while Sonya lay across my legs, exposed and watching us intently.

This was fun, but it was time for more. "Clothes off, both of you." I helped Sonya stand and watched them both as I stripped out of my own clothing. Seeing them bare and exposed was stunning.

115

If they were both a part of this, I was going to taste them both. I gripped the back of Jeremy's neck, and Sonya's gasp of delight was almost as loud as his groan. I crushed my mouth to his, and slipped my fingers between her legs, tasting his kisses and teasing her pussy.

I needed more. I needed to leave my past behind. Feel Sonya wrapped around my cock again and lose myself in her and Jeremy's bodies and minds.

13 /
sonya

I'd never lived anything like this. The intensity of the touches. The shared looks. The primal grunts and the atmosphere of desperate desire. It was like one of my books, but so much better because I was in the middle of it.

How fucking incredible was that?

Quentin faced me, his hands on my hips, and guided me with him as he stepped back to the couch. As he sat, he coaxed me to straddle his legs. He teased the head of his cock along my slit, but the sound rumbling from him said I wasn't the only one enjoying the sensation.

I gripped his shaft, taking control, and bumped my clit with his dick. It was meant to be a way to torture him, but it felt so good, and I was so close to orgasm. The longer I stroked him, the faster and harder I pressed him into me, using him as a human sex toy.

He gripped my thighs, digging his fingers in. *Goddess* I wanted him to mark me in so many ways.

I lost myself in the sensation, using his cock to tease my clit. Pumping and grinding as climax built inside me. Falling into the pleasure as orgasm washed over me.

When I finally slowed to a stop and opened my eyes, Quentin was watching me with a wild, terrifying look. He gripped my chin. "After that, I *need* to fuck you."

I rose as I scooted forward, and guided him inside me. The way he stretched me out sent anticipation humming through me. We rocked against each other in a slow motion that tantalized without doing more.

Jeremy brushed my hair from my neck and kissed up my shoulder to my earlobe. He nibbled the tender flesh. "Move so you're both sideways on the couch."

"Why?" I asked.

"Because I want my cock inside your tight, slick pussy at the same time as Quentin's."

Quentin groaned. "Fuuuuck."

His sliding out of me was a bittersweet blend of disappointment, and anticipation for what came next. He positioned himself sideways on the couch, and pulled my chest to his when he penetrated me again.

I was still slick and ready from the spanking and

teasing. Jeremy slid his fingers inside me, next to Quentin's dick.

Wow, that was differently delicious.

"Relax." Jeremy's voice was soft but commanding as he stretched my opening a little bit at a time. It was uncomfortable, but it felt incredible at the same time.

The intensity of the sensation was almost too much when Jeremy slid his cock inside me, nestled against Quentin. But knowing they rested against each other, pressed against my inner walls, made me slick all over again.

They rocked together in a slow build of friction. Jeremy worked his hand between us to find my clit. I was so turned on by the newness of this—the incredible blend of everything—it didn't take much to coax me toward orgasm again.

Clenching around them when I came was its own kind of ache and delight. It was almost too much, but at the same time I tumbled past the edge of uncomfortable and into the drawn-out intensity of a third climax.

Their groans mingled with my gasps. Quentin grunted and Jeremy panted and I had no idea which of them came first, but I swore I felt them spilling inside me.

Jeremy collapsed on me, sandwiching me between him and Quentin, while we caught our breath. Jeremy slid out of me first, and it was like being popped or deflated, in the best possible way.

Quentin withdrew from me as well, and pulled me into his lap as he sat. Jeremy settled beside us on the couch, and moved my legs to rest on his.

I wasn't the woman who got the guy. Especially not two of them. And I definitely wasn't the woman who broke the rules, like *no hooking up with your co-workers*. But here I was, sitting naked in my living room, wrapped up with two gorgeous men—my roommate and my co-worker.

Should I feel guilty? Not about what I did, but whom, and the fact that I wanted more when I wasn't part of the long-term plan.

I'd save guilt for later. I was basking now.

Jeremy pulled the crocheted throw from the back of the couch and draped it over all of us. "Now we don't have to go anywhere for a while."

Brilliant man.

"Let me see if I understand how this works," Quentin said.

I was missing a point of reference. "The blanket?"

Jeremy tugged one edge tighter. "If you make sure you're covered, it helps keep you warm and lets you ignore that you have no idea where half of your clothes landed."

"Smart asses. Both of you." Quentin laughed. "I meant this Rule 34 thing. If I wanted to play, I could say *Aliens*. The movie, not the History Channel guy."

"Too easy." Jeremy shook his head. "You've got androids, tentacles, and space suits. It's already practically porn without any work at all."

Quentin winced. "I do *not* want to know what's on your hard drive."

"Are you sure? You never know if you like it until you try it." Jeremy winked at Quentin.

They were so adorable when they flirted with each other.

Quentin turned to me. "Are you a tentacle girl?"

A question I'd put far more thought into over the years than most people would admit, especially since my boss—my mentor—at Rinslet was a woman with a tentacle fetish. "I don't see what the tentacles get out of it, but all those appendages working to get me off? There's an appeal in that. Besides, a Queen is female, so she probably has a good idea what a woman likes."

"I'm so very disturbed right now." Quentin's heavy sigh was exaggerated, but he snuggled closer to us. "But also far more curious than I should tell you."

"See?" Jeremy sounded smug.

"No. I don't see at all. Not that I'm owning up to, anyway. What about…" Quentin stalled.

I could almost hear the wheels turning, because

this same trap had caught me before. "Is there a problem?" I asked.

"This is a lot harder when I realize how fucked up the two of you are."

I grinned. "That used to trip me up, too, but I accepted my fucked-upness and rolled with it."

"Isn't it brilliant?" Jeremy trailed a finger lazily along my skin.

Quentin shrugged. "It's kind of hot, to be honest."

He and Jeremy were definitely flirting. A giddy bubble grew inside me at the thought of them as a cute, filthy couple. If I pushed them together a little more, would I lose this with them? The unwelcome thought deflated my joy. We shouldn't even be having sex, but I was already addicted to this new, physical part of our relationship.

"What about Evil Dead?" Quentin asked.

Which meant summoning ancient demons and depravity. Except Jeremy wasn't going to allow it.

"You win." Jeremy said. "I won't build porn around that."

Called it.

Quentin studied him, eyes narrowed. "With all the possibilities…"

"You can't make a perfect movie better, even with demon dick," Jeremy said.

"*Perfect movie.*" Quentin's voice was flat. "I can't

believe I let you touch my dick." He took his time extracting himself from us.

I grabbed his wrist and pulled him back into our mini puppy-pile. "Jeremy is a Bruce Campbell fanboy. Give him some leeway."

"You want porn? I'd let that man use and humiliate me." Jeremy was completely serious.

Quentin settled back in. "Watching that sounds far more appealing than the tentacles."

They were *so* good together.

"Totally unrelated—as fun as this is—you should come with us tomorrow," Jeremy said.

Quentin nodded. "I've become rather fond of coming with you."

I snorted a laugh. "Not what he meant."

"You're the word people—use your words. Be specific, or I'm going to go back to all the ways I want to see the two of you fucked."

Jeremy shook his head, but he was grinning. "My sisters and I volunteer once a month or so, and we've grown the group over the last few years. Sonya will be there. And Nigel. Tomorrow we're helping build a shelter, and an extra set of hands always makes the day go faster."

"That sounds great. I'm in," Quentin said.

So far, my plans for getting the two of them to hook up hadn't gone like I expected, but this was at least as good.

Someone knocked on the front door then rang

the bell. Weird. I never got unannounced visitors.

"I'll get it." Quentin successfully untangled himself from us this time. He pulled on his sweats and looked around the room. "I'll tell them they have the wrong house, and we can get back to coming together. Where the fuck is my shirt?" He grabbed a blanket off the back of a chair and draped it around his shoulders like a cape. "Don't go anywhere."

"Do you think your shower will fit three people?" Jeremy asked as Quentin strolled away.

I loved the motivation behind the suggestion. "Probably not. Besides, Art would remind you that shower sex is highly impractical."

"That's the fun in it." Jeremy grabbed his jeans and yanked them on, and then his shirt. He tossed me my clothes.

I didn't want to get dressed, but it was more practical than wandering around the house naked. I wasn't *that* comfortable with these two. "What do you think is taking him so long?"

Jeremy shrugged.

We padded toward the front door. As we neared the entryway, I heard a man's voice I didn't recognize say, "Please, just hear me out."

I turned the corner in time to see Quentin swing the door shut in the man's face without a reply.

"Who was that?" I asked.

Quentin didn't turn around. "My ex-husband."

14 /
quentin

My ex-husband was standing on the front porch, all but begging me to talk to him.

The man who bankrupted me. Destroyed my livelihood. Made it impossible for me to work in this city doing something I excelled at.

The man who broke my heart.

How was I supposed to react to his being here?

What I wanted to do was open the door again and deck him. Right cross to the jaw should bring him down hard. But then Sonya would have to deal with an unconscious man on her property, and regardless of my personal feelings, it was technically assault.

Besides, the last thing I wanted was for him to see how much he'd hurt me. He didn't fucking deserve that.

"I'll tell him to leave." Jeremy stepped toward me, reminding me I wasn't alone in the room.

I moved into Jeremy's path, blocking the door. "No. I've got this." I turned my attention to the door and opened it to face Mick again.

"Q. Thank God. I just—"

"Stop." I hated hearing him use that nickname as much as I hated him standing here, acting like I should want to hear anything he had to say. "Do you have the money you took?"

"No. But I—"

"Do you have a way to get the business back? To repay the clients you fucked over?"

"No."

"Goodbye, Mick." At least I got to say it this time. I let the door swing shut.

The cloud of rage lingered, and counting to ten wasn't going to fix anything. The way Sonya was watching me with what had to be intense pity... I couldn't deal with that.

"Quentin..."

"Please don't." I kept my voice kind. She wasn't trying to be cruel. "Whatever you're about to say, don't. I just need some time to clear my head."

Jeremy opened his mouth, but Sonya put a hand on his arm, silencing him. "Okay," she said.

I strode toward my room as quickly as I could without sprinting, yanked on a shirt and shoes, and grabbed my keys and phone. A moment later, I was on the road, pointing my car toward less traffic.

My hands itched to do more than hold a

steering wheel. I missed that outlet of welding—of creating something beautiful from a hunk of metal. I needed to prove to myself that despite everything Mick took from me, he couldn't have that.

There was one place I could go, though I hated to drop in on her with such little notice. I met Brooke years ago. She sculpted lead, and we frequented a lot of the same spots for supplies and tools when I was still working. Over the years, we'd become friends, and when Mick left me— before I knew Sonya or Jeremy—Brooke was about the only person who didn't turn her back on me.

She had a large shed on her property that she'd converted into a workshop, and she'd let me use it a few times. I didn't like to ask, and only did so when it might lead to work, but today I needed that tactile feeling.

I called her.

"Hey, stranger." Her tone was bright when she answered. "How've you been?"

"Fine. You know." It had been a while since I talked to her. How rude was I, only calling for a favor?

"I don't know unless you tell me," she teased. "And you don't sound fine. What's up?"

"Mick is back."

"Oh. I'm so sorry. What does he want?"

"I don't know. I didn't hear him out." And I was

less in the mood to tell her more than I was to talk to Sonya.

"Do you want to come by?" she asked.

A *no* formed at the back of my throat, even though that was why I'd called.

"You don't have to talk to me. You can use the shop if you want, and just lose yourself for a few hours," Brooke said. "Paige has a lot of scrap that I haven't figured out what I want to do with yet. You can dig your way through that."

Paige was her daughter and a talented mechanic. At seventeen, she had an instinct for vehicles that few people would ever achieve. She'd helped me keep my junker running when no one should've been able to breathe life into it.

And if I didn't take Brooke up on her offer, I was going to spend the next several hours growling and not getting anything done, and feel far worse at the end of the day. "I'd like that, yeah."

"Perfect. I'm finally allowed back on my feet after spraining my ankle, and this will give me an excuse to walk around."

"Pretty sure you're supposed to take it easy after that."

"Pft. You sound like everyone else. I'm not going line-dancing; I'm letting you into the workshop and saying *hi*."

"I'll be there in about thirty. And thank you."

"Anytime. You know that," Brooke said.

After *goodbyes* and hanging up, I headed toward the small town she lived in. Most of the valley had grown and merged into one continuous suburb over the decades, but this place was tucked away in the mountains, enough that it stayed small and isolated.

I wouldn't want to be there full time, but Brooke seemed to like it, and the quiet was nice every once in a while.

When I got to Brooke's, she was as bright and friendly as on the phone, unlocking her workshop for me and pointing me toward a fresh stack of scrap.

"I'd make small talk, but I doubt you're in the mood," she said.

I shook my head. "I'm really not."

"You know where everything is. Come find me if you need anything. Like an ear."

I gave her a tight smile. "Thank you."

When she was gone, I headed to the pile of scrap she'd pointed out. I had no idea what I was looking for, so I grabbed random pieces—sheet metal, rebar, pipes, and a few slabs I couldn't identify the previous purpose of.

Pulling on the safety gear—gloves, apron, visor—was soothing. A kind of familiar that let me fall into the ritual of it. And then I was cutting and shaping and welding.

The shed had some climate control, but not a lot, and the cold air, combined with the high heat of the torch, required more focus than I'd need on a hot day. It was a welcome distraction.

Not enough of one, though. Every time I paused, my mind drifted back to Mick, asking me to hear him out. Which summoned the pain and rage of when I woke up to him being gone.

And the blame... It always started with my calling him a selfish bastard and slid to my asking myself why I didn't see it coming. We'd had a few problems as a couple, but not a lot. Not the kind of shouting matches that some of our friends had. Our arguments were about money—as in how much he tended to lose when he took weekend trips to Wendover.

He'd gotten help, though. Gone through treatment and dealt with the gambling addiction. I'd seen him falter more than once, but I thought he was handling it. Which meant I chose to ignore that we talked less and less as time went on. His late nights should've been work. Yeah, I was the sucker who bought that line.

I was the fucking idiot who'd missed all the signs.

I didn't know how long Brooke had been standing there when I looked up from my work.

"You were focused. I didn't want to startle you," she said.

The door was open behind her, and the sun was low in the sky. "What time is it?" I asked.

"Four. I have to go out in about half an hour, but you can lock up when you're done."

I'd been here for hours and not realized it. I shook the clouds away from my thoughts. "No. I should get going too."

"That's gorgeous." She nodded at my work. "Is it based on something?"

I hadn't been paying attention, but apparently, it was a 3D representation of the logo from the game Sonya and Jeremy were a part of. Based on what I knew about Brooke, probably not her kind of game. "Something that reminds me of friends."

"Well, I love it."

"Thanks. I'll get out of your hair. Just give me a few to clean up."

"No worries. You know where to find me." Brooke waved and walked out of the shed.

I cleaned up quickly, making sure everything was back where it belonged.

Brooke came back out to chat with me as I was loading the two-foot sculpture into my car. When an old pickup truck pulled into the driveway and parked a few feet from us, her attention left me completely.

The man who climbed out of the older Ford truck had tattoos peeking up from under his collar, and his hair was cut close to his scalp. Not quite regulation, but close. He looked me over as he approached.

I bit back the desire to say, *I'm way too old to train a young boyfriend*. No telling how that kind of joke would land, and thinking it reminded me of how unceremoniously I'd walked out on Sonya and Jeremy.

"Deacon. Hey." Brooke's smile for him was solar systems brighter than the ones she gave me. "This is Quentin."

"Pleasure." I extended my hand. "Where did you serve?"

His grip was tighter than it needed to be when we shook. "Denny's, for about two weeks in high school? Waiting tables wasn't for me."

"Ah." I chuckled. "I assumed…" I scrubbed my hand over my own short hair.

"No. Never military. Much respect, though." Deacon sounded sincere, if not begrudging.

Brooke angled herself half-between us. "He did a charity stream with a friend for Christmas and had to shave his head as part of it. A Konsoles for Kids thing."

I was impressed. "Cool."

"Thanks." Deacon's voice was tight.

If Brooke was fucking this guy—which either was the case or they both wanted it to be—I hoped she was prepared for a little immaturity. "Great to meet you, Deacon. And I'll see you around, Brooke."

"Remember, you're always welcome." She gave me a quick hug, while Deacon scowled behind her.

As I headed home, my thoughts rebounded quickly to the people waiting for me. *Person?* Was Jeremy still there? The last few days with him and Sonya had been more fun, more real, than anything I'd done in a long time. The road trip. The sex. The hanging out.

I was looking forward to tomorrow and to seeing their reactions when I showed them what I'd made.

But Mick's being back was a cloud over all of it. A brutal reminder that I couldn't afford to get comfortable in any relationship. Friendship was pushing it, and romance?

Nope. Couldn't do it.

The last thing I was going to do was surrender my heart to another person.

Never again.

15 /
jeremy

Quentin's ex's surprise visit killed the mood in Sonya's house. She and I worked our way through a few more pages of screenplay notes, but when Quentin didn't come back for a few hours, it was obvious she was more worried about him than getting things done.

She eventually sent me home and promised to call if she needed anything.

She sent a text about an hour later. *He's home, but quiet.*

Knowing Sonya, she was worried and trying not to hover around him to see how she could help.

Do you want me to come back, I asked. Distract her. Remind her she had me. Pretend I had no idea how I wanted Quentin to fit into any of that.

No, but thanks. We'll see you tomorrow.

I'd seen Sonya almost every day for years, but tonight the simple promise made me smile.

When she'd brought up the arbor for Megan's wedding, I figured out what Sonya was up to with her *blacksmithing quest*. She was looking for a way to get him back into welding that he wouldn't be able to turn down, and for some reason she was hiding the brainstorming behind the idea of *let's make a quest.*.

A bit convoluted, but it was why I'd invited him to join us tomorrow. He may or may not make a contact to help him get back on his feet, career-wise, but there was a better chance than if he stayed home

Besides, the last week had been a lot of fun. Sure, the kisses with Quentin started for Sonya's sake—not that I minded, the physical was fantastic with him—but I was enjoying his company almost as much as hers. The sex today. The other morning. In the hotel…

What if the three of us were more? Obviously it could work; I knew multiple people in three way relationships.

But not us.

Quentin was emotionally unavailable. Sonya was struggling with her insecurities. And last time I decided *maybe we should make this more*, I fucked things up with a good friend. I eventually not only lost my friendship with the woman I'd married, but because we had so many friends in common, our divorce hurt them too.

I couldn't do that again. I couldn't risk taking things to the next level with Sonya. Writing romance was one thing, but recognizing actual love?

I wasn't willing to take a chance guessing.

When I got to the worksite Sunday morning, a handful of volunteers were already there. Megan and Nigel stood near a table set up with coffee and pastries, away from most everyone else.

Since we were kids, our parents had made us spend at least one day a month doing something to help other people. When Megan, Carly, and I were younger, we hated that the activity took away from our lives. But we all learned to appreciate it as we hit adulthood.

Even though our parents moved to Arizona a few years ago, when they retired, my sisters and I still maintained the tradition. This week we were working for a group building a tiny home community for the homeless. I was surprised to see Megan here, but not that her fiancé was absent.

Sonya had this ideal about people and love, and I wouldn't deny that my perspective was twisted compared to hers, but Megan's fiancé really was a Grade A asshole. He'd been working for months to separate her from friends and family. He convinced her to miss Sonya's bestselling author celebration, and for me that was a top of the line *what the fuck* kind of thing.

But Megan was here today, and everyone else was arriving as well. This was going to be fun.

I introduced Carly to Quentin, and the appraising look she gave him was the same one she gave a gorgeous property she couldn't wait to explore. A sharp *hands off* echoed in my thoughts, and I buried it.

Sonya and Nigel talked to the organizer, and they were back quickly with instructions and to hand out assignments. We were hanging Sheetrock in a handful of the houses.

Quentin shouldered the sheets into place while Carly secured them, and the rest of us taped and mudded in.

With all six of us working, a room didn't take long. We did the first two with minimal discussion beyond Nigel and Sonya directing us.

By Room Three, we had our rhythm.

"So, Nigel," Quentin said between the grunts of lifting a full piece of sheetrock by himself. "How did you get into knife throwing?"

"I grew up in the circus."

Quentin's laugh died when he looked at Nigel's serious, stern face.

I rolled my eyes, knowing what came next.

Nigel's scowl shifted to a smirk in a heartbeat. "I

know, right? No one expects an answer like that, but it's true."

"I assume there's more to the story." Quentin leaned into the board, and Carly screwed it into place with practiced efficiency.

Nigel placed the tape along the seam. "I mean, yeah?"

"His parents were the acrobatic performance and they were killed by a mob boss when he was thirteen." Sonya filled in screw holes. "A brooding billionaire took pity on him and adopted him."

Quentin paused long enough to shoot her a raised eyebrow. "Pretty sure that's Batman."

"Oh my God, you're Dick Grayson and you never told us?" Megan's squeal was over the top.

"You tell people you wear those sexy green and yellow tights, and then everyone wants to see you in them, and he has more important things to do." I picked up Sonya's story.

Quentin shook his head and let out a heavy sigh. "Yeah, yeah. You all know the story. I don't." Despite that, he was smiling.

"Real story is boring," Nigel said. "I was born into a family of performers, I had a knack for knives, and when I got older I decided I wanted more from life and I left.

Megan pressed her arm to his, probably closer than she needed to, as she applied mud to the tape he laid down. "Leave it to Nigel to do things differently than everyone else and run away *from* the circus."

"I'm more of a *use my mind* person than a *subject myself to a lifetime of humiliation* person." Nigel lingered next to Megan after he finished.

Was I looking for things that were there? "Which explains his sex life."

"He said as if that were a bad thing," Sonya added her narration.

Megan blew out a soft *pft.* "Because my brother is a twisted fuck."

"Just a humiliated one, and only in the bedroom," Quentin offered.

We were all adults and my sisters and I hadn't shied away from certain topic for years, but I didn't appreciate that I'd become the focus of this particular joke. "I'm just saying, if Nigel can use his brain to make people orgasm…"

"One hundred percent your department," Nigel said. "Unless we're talking Jedi mind control. Still working on that."

Megan nudged him playfully. "Let me know how that goes."

"You're not coming, so I'm not there yet."

I was dim sometimes, but this was pretty obvious. "Did you just imply you're trying to Jedi mind-fuck my sister?"

Megan shot me a look that could've withered the Sheetrock mud. "Mind fuck, really?"

She was right—that was her fiancé's job. I kept the thought to myself and gave her what I hoped was an apologetic shrug.

The conversation moved to less loaded topics.

When we broke for lunch, the entire group of volunteers met back at the starting point. I grabbed a box with a sandwich and chips, and went to join my friends.

Carly stepped in my path. "Starting to feel like a sixth wheel here."

"Pretty sure that's not how the saying goes, and maybe you should be having this conversation with Megan."

"Tell me Nigel's not a better choice than that jackass she's seeing," Carly said. "And I'm not talking about them."

I shook my head. "I don't know what you're talking about."

"Megan is going to be furious if you break Sonya's heart."

The words tightened like a band around my chest, tying the past to the present. "I'm not—"

"Fucking her?" Carly asked. "I don't want to know."

"Sonya is one of my best friends. For years now."

"This is different."

Was it obvious or was she just fishing for details?

"You're imagining things." So was I, because I wanted to see what she did. It wasn't there, though.

She shook her head. "Okay, Goober. Except that everyone but you knows you've loved her for as long as you've known her."

"You're definitely wrong about that." I didn't fall. Not for Sonya or Quentin or anyone.

16 /
sonya

The wind kicked up in the early afternoon, and the people running the project decided to shut everything down for the day and send volunteers home.

"You're welcome back at my place." The way Jeremy tossed the casual suggestion out felt natural. "Both of you."

Which was good, since Quentin and I rode to the work site together, but made me wonder if Jeremy only invited me so it wouldn't be obvious he was inviting Quentin.

We all agreed it was a good idea, especially since our afternoon plans were cancelled, and the three of us headed to Jeremy's.

His house was in an older part of the city, and sat on about an acre of land. The garage he used was newer and next to his house, but there was a second building, a detached carriage house, further back on the property.

When I stepped into his house, and actual light hit me, rather than the blustery day that had blown in, or the sunlight that filtered through windows earlier, I realized this might have been a mistake. "I'm covered in dust and mud."

Quentin raised his fingers to the top of my head and my body clenched in anticipation when he brushed along my scalp. He trailed his touch down a short distance before pulling away with a small piece of plaster in his hand.

I mentally laughed at myself. It wasn't like I could expect him to pull my hair and kiss me like I was a lifeline every time he was nearby.

Jeremy pulled his shirt away from his skin and let go. "I always forget how much sweating can happen, even when it's barely above freezing outside."

"No offense, but I am starting to wonder why we didn't go home and clean up." Quentin scrubbed his hand across his head and plaster dust floated free and to the ground.

"You could've done that, but *I* have a shower big enough for three people," Jeremy said.

I liked what he was implying but, "Why do I feel like we were set up?"

Jeremy shrugged. "I'd like to claim I thought of it beforehand, but my foresight isn't nearly that good." He tugged at the hem of my shirt. "You can go, if you want."

"I do not want." Instead of pulling away, I stepped closer to Jeremy.

Quentin pressed into my back. "If the shower is here, and the two of you are in the shower, I'm in the right place."

I needed to keep in mind that my goal was to push the two of them together, but I wasn't interested in turning Jeremy down. Every time his fingers brushed my skin, tantalizing chills rolled through me. Combined with the heat radiating from Quentin, and I was hooked. I had to have this. Have them.

I was startled in the best possible way when Jeremy tightly gripped my wrists. "I want to see you pinned down." The command in his voice was delicious. "I want to see you restrained, squirming in pleasure, and hear you screaming my name when you come on my fingers and my cock."

Goddess, I wanted that too.

He pushed my arms behind me, and Quentin caught me and held me tight.

I couldn't take my eyes off Jeremy as heat and anticipation spilled through me.

His bite on my bottom lip morphed to a hard kiss that ached with desperation in my soul and cranked my desire past its limit.

"You can do whatever you want to me," I repeated the promise from the other day.

He shook his head and smirked. "That's a long list. Let's start with a sampler." He shoved my top up over my head without ever jarring me from Quentin's grip. The action tugged at my hair and stretched out my shirt and left me even more restrained.

So. Incredible.

Jeremy yanked my bra up as well, cupped one breast, and wrapped his mouth around my nipple. While he sucked and flicked the hard nub with his tongue and teeth, Quentin bit along my neck and shoulder. Nibbled at my earlobe. Covered me in kisses and bite marks.

They continued the layers of attention until need was pulsing non-stop between my legs and I had to squeeze my thighs together. Not that gesture did anything but amplify my desire.

"This is torture." I tried to keep my tone light despite my gasps for breath between each tease.

Jeremy's smirk grew. "That's the point."

"Do you want me to beg?" I asked.

"Without question." Jeremy raised his head and his gaze penetrated my soul. "I want to hear you whimper and beg and scream my name when you come. And I want to know you mean it."

"I want that too." So very much.

This was the Jeremy who wrote vividly sexy

scenes at work. The guy who gave me some of my naughtier ideas for sex scenes in books. This wasn't the Jeremy who casually hung out with me like a friend...

But it was, and Goddess, I would never forget again that he was capable of such delicious things.

He shoved my jeans and panties to the floor, leaving them around my ankles and putting me on display as Quentin held me in place.

"You're so gorgeous." The way Jeremy looked me over, I felt like a priceless display. "Gorgeous mind. Gorgeous body." He cupped my breast and pinched a nipple hard enough to both hurt and delight me. "Gorgeous fucking pussy." He danced his fingers between my legs, lightly teasing the skin.

His sudden penetration stretched me out and stole my breath.

Quentin captured both my wrists with one powerful hand, and moved the other to my breast to roll a nipple between his fingers, while Jeremy pumped his hand inside of me. He hooked his fingers up, and teased his thumb over my clit.

Jeremy pushed me to the edge of orgasm, then edged away before I came. Again and then again. Between his attention and Quentin's, I was gasping with need.

"Please let me come. *Goddess*, please." The words rasped past my lips.

Jeremy's wicked grin was almost enough to push

me over the edge, and the way he pressed into my clit, harder and faster, yanked orgasm from me He kept stroking and teasing until it was almost too much. But it felt so good.

When he finally pulled away, he and Quentin were the only reason I stayed upright on wobbly legs. Jeremy sucked on his slick fingers, licking my juices from them. With me sandwiched between them, he leaned into Quentin for a kiss, and to share my taste.

So. Fucking. Hot.

"We should see about that shower." Quentin's voice was as rough as my stance.

"I'm not sure I can make it to the bathroom." I was only half-joking.

I squealed when Quentin scooped me into his arms and carried me through the house, following Jeremy. I draped my arms around his neck. "A girl could get used to this."

"And you should be able to," he said.

He made sure I was steady when he set me down near the shower. The three of us finished undressing, and seeing the two of them help each other out of their clothes was its own flavor of arousing.

Jeremy made sure the water was the right temperature and we stepped into a surround-water experience of shower jets.

For a short while, we managed to soap and wash

each other. It was tender and sensual, with Quentin's hands gliding over Jeremy's body, and Jeremy massaging my scalp as he washed my hair.

I spent extra time soaping up their cocks, and in return Quentin lingered with his fingers between my legs.

The space wasn't quite big enough to maneuver, but the three of us managed. When Jeremy slipped between us and behind me, I was curious. When he captured my wrists again, I gasped in surprise and delight. He pinned my hands behind my back and pressed my front to the wall. The tile was cool against my skin and his touch was fire, sizzling as the shower rained on us from multiple angles.

His cock dug into my ass while his fingers dug into my skin. "I need to feel your tight, wet pussy wrapped around my cock." He growled. "Squeezing me until I spill inside you."

He slipped along my skin, and thrust inside me without further warning, making me cry out.

With the side of my face flat against the wall, I had the perfect view of Quentin stroking himself while he watched us, his breathing heavy and his eyes lidded with lust.

Jeremy hammered inside me hard and fast. The intensity of his grip and raw need in his movements had me hovering on the edge of climax and the way Quentin watched us pushed me into orgasm.

I lost myself in the sensations when I came, letting pleasure rip from my throat in raw cries.

Quentin came in short, heavy grunts, squirting across my hip and thigh.

Jeremy increased his pace, hammering against me with raw abandon, his breathing stopping for a heartbeat, before he let out a long groan and finished.

For a moment, the only sounds in the room were the shower and us trying to catch our breath. We all leaned into each other, our weight being the only thing keeping us upright.

We finished showering, helped each other dry off, and crawled into Jeremy's bed in a cuddly pile.

This wouldn't last, what the three of us had right now, but for tonight it was incredible.

Monday morning I had an appointment with Dominic to discuss the rights contracts I'd received so far. I didn't have any meetings at work, so I'd asked Jeremy to cover for me for a few hours.

As I was walking out the door, a text came in from Jeremy. *Miss you until you get here.*

Where did that come from? It didn't matter, because it left warm fuzzies fluttering inside anyway.

Dominic's law office was downtown, only a few blocks from the AcesPlayed building. I had no idea what to expect from this meeting, but I was shown to a meeting room almost immediately, and he joined me a moment later. He was dressed in an impeccable suit and held himself like a man who knew he owned the room.

His handshake was firm and reinforced his presence of *you want me on your side.* And I did.

"Congratulations on your rapid rise to fame." He sounded sincere.

I still wasn't sure I'd call it fame, but considering thousands more people knew my name now than two weeks ago, it was probably true. "Thank you."

"I've looked over the contracts you sent me. From now on, all of this communication will go through me." Dominic took the seat next to me, opened a tablet, and set it up between us so I could see the screen.

"I understand." And preferred things that way.

He unlocked the device and pulled up a document that looked a lot like a contract. "Before we go through this, is there anything you're hoping to get from this that you didn't see in the contracts? This is the first conversation about what you want, not the last, so don't feel like you need to think of all of it right now."

"Creative input. That is… if you think it's possible?"

"Anything's possible. In your case, it may even be probable. Is that a deal breaker?"

No. The conversation with Quentin and Jeremy flooded back, about the details I shouldn't concede to my mother about my story. "There are details I won't allow to be changed. So creative control isn't a deal breaker, but I'd like input, and if those things aren't included, I'm out."

"Good to know." He flipped to a different screen and made a note before coming back to the contract he'd opened. "Anything else?"

"Maybe? Probably? Not that I know of right now."

"Okay. Let's talk about what I'm seeing here."

For the next hour, we went through each contract. He pointed out concerns and suggestions. Asking for a percent of net instead of gross, retaining merchandise rights, control over the source material, and several other terms I'd heard my mom toss around but that I never would've thought to look for myself.

"I'm so glad I called you," I said as he moved from contract three to four.

"Of course you are." He didn't have to scroll far in the Epithet Romance contract. "I've never worked with them before, but I've heard stories from colleagues. They're notoriously unyielding and going through this… I see a lot of rights grabs in this line of work, but this is more of a kidnapping with assault and battery."

Ouch. "Is this their boilerplate contract?" I

wanted to believe my mom had made certain concessions before she even sent me the offer, but she was so anti-nepotism I'd felt the whiplash of her *no* when I applied for an internship with her during college.

"If it's not I'd hate to see worse, but I suspect it is." He went through pages of things that needed to be removed before I even considered their offer. "The name on this, Mary Russel... relative?"

"My mother."

"Take or leave this advice, but in my experience doing business like this with family is a mistake more often than not."

My mom may not think much of my writing, but she was intelligent, driven, and one of the best at her jobs. I bristled at the recommendation. "I'll keep that in mind." My reply came out more coolly than I intended.

"All right." His expression and tone never changed. I bet he was one hell of a poker player. "Keep in mind a lot of these conversations should be kept between us and the contracting companies. Don't go discussing details with other people."

"Everyone at work knows I have offers, but not details."

"That's fine. Keep it at that, and they'll understand."

We covered a few more things, he promised to send all revisions to me before they went back to the different production companies, and I left his office feeling good about what he had to say.

I checked my phone on the way to my car, to find two new text messages. The one from Jeremy said, *It's all hands on when you get in. Fair warning, everyone's freaking out.*

Well shit.

The second message was from Judith. *The instant you're here, come see me.*

Double shit.

There were also email notifications from my mom's assistant, and a huge podcaster whose show I loved. Both were requests that I get back to them soon, and as much as I itched to do that, I needed to know what was going on at work.

Fortunately it was a short drive.

"I'll tell her you're on your way back," Ivan greeted me as soon as I walked in the front door.

I cut a straight line to Judith's office to find her waiting for me, a sterner look than normal on her face. She never looked out of place or frazzled, but today she was a fraction closer.

She gestured to a chair. "How was the meeting with Dominic?"

Hardly important at this very moment. "Good. Can't say much more."

"Figured. Fallyn found a massive exploit in the game and this morning she broadcast it to the world."

Triple shit. Jackpot. "Fuck."

"Precisely. Though, we're grateful she found it now while we're in beta, and not a year from now. The game's offline until we fix and test it."

Story wasn't typically involved in things like that. Not that we had an issue with helping, but it wasn't our area of expertise. "What do you need us to do?"

"Dev has already located the problem," Judith said. "Apparently Fallyn emailed us the details a few weeks ago, and the information sat in someone's inbox unopened, because it had her name on it. She included error logs, exact steps to reproduce it, and theories on where the issue stemmed from."

I'd ask *whose inbox*, but I could guess and his name started with *Chris* and ended with *is still a misogynistic asshole*. "At least that's something."

"It will take the whole company to help test. Everyone's priority this week is playing the portions of the game that Nigel assigns, thoroughly, to make sure we're good. Everyone else is already in the big conference room."

Which included Jeremy, based on his text. So why was I getting the personal drill down of the situation? "I'll get started if that's all?"

"It's not."

My gut twisted in on itself, even though I expected her response.

"What's happening to you right now is amazing.

Once in a lifetime shit, and *fuck* this is hard for me to say, because you know how I feel about pursuing dreams."

Squash anything in your path and sacrifice whatever you must to get there. I nodded.

"I won't ask you to turn down or ignore or damage any opportunities coming your way. You deserve what's happening right now, and you need to take advantage of it."

"Okay…?" I couldn't begin to guess where this was going.

"But I need someone doing this work this week. I need every person on this. If you aren't sure you can do that, tell me now so I can bring in a temp or make other arrangements. Bowing out now won't hurt your job, but I need to know."

I couldn't let the team down and my contract negotiations would move slowly. "I'm yours for the week."

"Thank you."

As I headed to the conference room, I sent Quentin a text letting him know I'd be home late all week.

I'll miss you. Let me know if you need anything.

Two *miss yous* in one day, from the two men I was trying to push toward each other. I didn't know if I wanted them to be *just friendly* messages or not.

The big room had been transformed to hold a series of long tables, and everyone else with the company was either already seated in front of their laptops, or walking the room. This was a similar setup to what we'd had the first day we launched our beta, but the mood was much more somber today.

I took a seat between Jeremy and Luna, across from Art. Jeremy squeezed my knee, never looking up from his own game.

It was going to be a long week that would feel even longer if I didn't figure out what I wanted from him. From Quentin.

17 /
quentin

By Thursday, I missed Sonya a lot more than I expected. And Jeremy. Sure, she and I didn't hang out all the time, but she was home many nights and the two of us put in a bit of time in front of the TV just having fun.

It was lonely with her leaving for work early, and coming home late exhausted with barely enough energy to collapse into bed. And seeing Jeremy so often last week…

I hadn't expected to miss someone's company again the way I did theirs. Not that it was the same as with Mick. She was a friend. Jeremy was a friend of a friend.

Usually I'd have work to keep my mind occupied, but I did a lot of one-off construction jobs and this time of year they weren't consistent. I spent the morning cleaning the house—not that it needed it and not that I had to, but it gave me something to do. By early afternoon, I was tapped for ideas. I could head to the library.

My phone rang, and I reached for it, grateful for the distraction. Mick's new number taunted me, and I scowled.

"What?" Why did I answer?

What else was I going to do?

"Please." Mick made the word sound as sincere as anything. Not that I was surprised. "Meet me for a late lunch. Give me half an hour."

Maybe it would give me closure. I doubted it, but I was spinning my wheels regardless. Maybe this would be a chance to take my frustration out on him instead. "All right."

A short while later, I arrived at the restaurant Mick picked. It was one of those that couldn't decide if it was family-style dining or a sports bar, and this time of day, the parking lot was mostly empty. As I approached the entrance, Mick was already waiting. As I drew within hearing distance, I opened my mouth to remind him this needed to be short and sweet.

"I'm sorry." He cut me off.

"I've heard that before."

"And I always thought I meant it."

So this was going to happen the way it had in the past. "And yet, here we are."

Mick raked his fingers through his hair—dark strands long enough to brush the top of his ears, that I'd always told him was too long. He was positively shaggy compared to Jeremy.

"I'm not here to try to win you back," Mick said. "I'm here to apologize. Talk if you're willing to listen. But the apology is the important part."

"Why? Are you on Step Nine right now?"

Mick nodded. "Yes."

I rolled my eyes and let out a heavy sigh. I'd seen him go through recovery before, for his gambling addiction. There was always a relapse, and he got better at hiding it each time.

"But also because you deserve an apology," he said. "Have lunch with me, You're here, it'll be easier to sit and talk than to stand out here and do it…"

I wasn't interested in making things easier on him. "All right." I wasn't sure why I agreed.

We headed inside, the lack of other customers reflecting the emptiness of the parking lot outside, and a waitress showed us to a booth near the back. She took our drink orders and left us alone.

"You look good." Mick's tone was casual.

Not what I was interested in. "Hmm."

"How have you been?"

"Seriously?" I looked at him in disbelief. "I'm in debt up to my fucking eyeballs, I can't get licensed again, and even if I could, no one's going to hire me. Not after I had to leave so many people fucked, thanks to you. How do you think I'm doing?"

This time Mick was the one who sighed.

But thank fuck he didn't try to initiate more conversation.

Our waitress returned with our drinks and asked if we were ordering. I wasn't, but Mick asked her for the same appetizer platter we always used to get, and two plates.

I didn't know what this was or why I was here. This wasn't the closure I thought I might find.

"I was going to call the woman you're staying with—Sonya?—to see if she could get you to talk to me. I thought that might piss you off more, though."

I glared at Mick, my fury surging white-hot. "If you go near her…"

"That wasn't a threat." Mick held up his hands. "I know it came out as one, but my point is I've been trying to figure out how to talk to you."

"And yet, you're not saying anything concrete. How did you find me, by the way? How do you know her name?" My last question came out on a growl.

Mick looked surprised. "A friend of hers tagged you in a photo, but it tagged our old shared account instead. She was easy enough to look up. I'm not stalking you."

"You're not winning me over or convincing me of anything." Except to ask Sonya's co-workers to be more careful with what they shared online.

The food arrived. The scents of spices, fried cheese, and grease churned my stomach. Mick gestured to the large plate and I shook my head.

He placed some of each on his own plate, but didn't eat. "I've rehearsed this so many times, and no version feels right." He dragged in a deep breath. "Here goes. I know I fucked you over and that I can never make up for what happened. I'm sorry anyway, but I don't expect your forgiveness. I gambled us to a point where I owed some scary people a lot of money—apparently that actually happens in real life—and I didn't realize how much it was going to hurt you until I hit rock bottom."

"Back then I would've gone through anything with you. Even that." I wasn't sure why I was admitting that, but saying the words lifted some weight from my chest.

"You shouldn't have had to."

He had that right. "No, but you were my husband and I loved you and I would've done it anyway. But now…"

"Like I said, I'm not trying to win you back. We're done. I accept that. But I don't want what I did to hurt who you are going forward. I don't want to cast this shadow over anyone else you meet. I'm an addict and I fucked up. Not everyone is like me."

I clucked and shook my head. "Enough people are that it's not worth the risk." I was done here. "I'm glad you're taking the right steps, and I hope for your sake that it sticks this time, but it doesn't change what you did to me or how I feel about it now." I walked out of the restaurant.

Leaving Mick behind didn't mean I could push the encounter from my thoughts, but replaying the conversation wasn't getting me anywhere. There was something I needed to grasp, and I couldn't quite reach it.

When the doorbell rang later that evening, I was still mulling things over. If that was Mick again, he could go fuck himself.

I opened to door, those words on my lips, and stalled when I found myself face to face with a woman who looked like an older version of Sonya, in much more expensive clothing. "I'd like to speak to Sonya, please."

"She's not here right now." I was already on edge and the way she looked me over with disdain made my neck tighten.

"I see. I didn't realize she was seeing someone."

And who the hell are you that you care? I shouldn't ask that if this was her mother, which was what I assumed. I was tempted to say *she's seeing two someones and she's never been fucked better*, but that wasn't my place. "I rent a room from her."

"And she lets you wander around her house while she's at work? She must trust you a great deal."

I was almost choking on this person's disdain. "May I help you?"

"I'm Mary Russel," she said. "I'm here to see my daughter and she said she'd be home soon. I'll wait." She stepped past me without waiting for an invitation.

Sonya would've called or texted if she was expecting a guest and didn't think she'd get here in time. Unless she was too busy. But why would her mother lie?

I didn't like anything about this.

18 /
jeremy

By Thursday at about five in the evening, everyone in the office was the kind of exhausted that resembled being drunk. The developers were working on the most recent round of revisions and the rest of us were waiting.

I needed something to keep me awake. "Rule 34."

Phillip groaned. "No. Please. I don't have enough energy to fuck right now."

"I'm sorry." Luna patted Adrienne's shoulder.

Adrienne giggled. "What? Like any of us do?"

"Also, hate to be the wet blanket here—"

"But do you really?" Luna cut Nigel off.

He glared at her. "Rule 34 is probably inappropriate at work."

"Since when?" Dustin asked.

"Probably since always, for normal people." Adrienne tried to stifle a yawn and lost the struggle.

"Fortunately, none of us are normal." Her tone shifted to drowsy as she lay her head on Dustin's shoulder.

The two of them and Phillip were lucky they got the in-office fucking, and the actual relationship out of the way before the new rules. They were also lucky they were so good together.

I snuck a glance at Sonya. I wouldn't dare risk our friendship, our working relationship, to pretend we could have something like Phillip, Dustin, and Adrienne, even if the temptation was there.

Dustin twisted his head to kiss Adrienne on the forehead without jarring her. "Okay, different game. A year after the zombie apocalypse—five things you always have with you when you leave camp."

"A condom," Danny said.

Nigel's sigh was heavy and exaggerated. "We just agreed no sex talk. And it's the fucking zombie apocalypse."

"This isn't sex talk, it's about protection," Danny argued. "And I know what it is, that's why I'm strapping one on while I'm fucking."

Luna scrubbed her face. Her eyes were ringed with smudged eyeliner and she looked like an adorable red headed raccoon. "But you're leaving camp."

I was pretty sure that was Danny's point. "Exactly. You don't know who has what out there. It's not like there's anyplace to get tested."

"So don't fuck random people your meet in your supply run." Nigel made it sound like his answer was the obvious answer.

Maybe in the real world.

"I can't believe I'm saying this, but I agree with Nigel." Luna sounded disappointed in herself. "You're going on a supply run. Do that and then get back to safety."

"Whoa." Dustin dragged out the word. "Am I in Looking Glass land? Where's the Cheshire Cat?"

"Alys is with the other devs." Adrienne offered helpfully.

"But Luna and Nigel just agreed on something." Phillip pinched Dustin, who made a noise much more like a groan than a yelp. "Nope. Not dreaming,.."

Luna sat forward, her expression determined. "Because survival is more important than fucking during a zombie apocalypse."

"But it's been a year," I teased. Despite the light arguing, everyone was smiling, even Luna and Nigel. This was fun.

"Which means you've had a year to find your-self a real girlfriend or boyfriend," Danny said.

"Oh." Adrienne sat straight up. "I have the world's last inflatable sheep. Her name's Baahtty. You don't need a condom for her. A year? Really? You poor thing."

I glanced at Sonya.

She raised her brows and turned to Luna. "What are you grabbing, then?"

"The one-handed military axe I have a special holster for." Luna may have put more thought into this than the rest of us combined.

Nigel pointed at her. Except him. "What she said. And the leather jacket I keep near the bed."

"Arm protection. Smart." Luna tapped the side of her head. "Also, a can opener."

Elliot had joined us. That must mean he had news. "This is starting to feel like a supply run and not a sex run." Or not.

"And honestly, it's starting to sound pretty serious," Phillip said.

The sound Luna made was somewhere between a sigh and a growl. "It's the zombie apocalypse. It's serious by default."

"You get to bring your fist," Nigel said. "By default. I bet it doesn't even have to be one of your five things. Does it?" He looked at Dustin.

Dustin shook his head. "Does not count toward the list, because you can't leave it behind in favor of something else. Or rather, you shouldn't."

"Are you sure? I'm starting to wonder with you people." Nigel sounded exasperated, but he was grinning.

"You're all ridiculous. Thank God," Elliot said.

Dustin held up two fingers. "You get two more things. Might as well finish the list."

Luna and Nigel stared at each other for a moment, lips pursed and brows furrowed. They both nodded.

Creepy. But also hilarious. I almost let a giggle slip out, though I wasn't sure why.

"Water," Luna said.

"Exactly," Nigel agreed. "Something to drink that you know is safe"

Luna sighed. "And I guess if you have to…"

"A condom." Nigel relented.

"*Yes,*" I said at the same time as Danny. We high-fived each other.

The room erupted in giggles that grew until we were all gasping for breath. It wasn't quite this funny, but I couldn't stop and it looked like I wasn't the only one.

"You should all go home." Elliot managed between snorts of laughter and gasps for air.

Dustin managed to bring himself under control. "It's barely six."

The laughter faded in the room. My cheeks ached and my eyes burned, but I'd missed this kind of connection with the team.

I looked at Sonya again and the bright pink of amusement coloring her cheeks. The laughter sparkling in her eyes. I had this with her even when no one else was around. I was so lucky.

"The next development step is going to take us a while," Elliot said. "We're tag-teaming the code."

"Good thing you brought the condoms," Sonya snorted.

And then we were all laughing again.

"No. Really. Go home," Elliot said when the noise died again. "Be back early, because we're going to need extra eyes on this work. I guarantee you the devs don't make much more sense than all of you."

"He said as if we made sense to begin with." I channeled Sonya.

She grinned. "That's what she said."

Elliot shook his head. "Go. Home."

With the mental stimulation gone, exhaustion settled into the room quickly. Everyone packed up in silence, and trickled out of the room in groups of one to three.

I watched Sonya shove her laptop into her messenger bag, then yank on her fingerless gloves—the pair with quotes from *The Raven* on them. An unfamiliar ache pinged in my chest. She was going home. To Quentin. And I was going back to my house, with nothing and no one to keep me company except empty rooms and that big, empty carriage house on the back of the property—

Inspiration struck. Holy shit, it was perfect. I fell into step beside Sonya as we headed outside. "I have a brilliant idea," I said at the same time she did.

"You first." Her smile was tired but bright.

"Okay, so you know that big garage on the back

of my lot? We should set that up so Quentin can work there."

Sonya squealed. "That is brilliant. Yay." She threw her arms around my neck.

I should let this be a quick hug, but her warm body molded to mine, and I wanted to hold her here for an eternity. To claim her mouth. To make her do more than squeal.

"What was your idea," I asked huskily.

She leaned more of her weight against me. "You should come back to my place, tell Quentin yourself, and then we see what happens from there." Her voice was soft.

At the loud sound of someone clearing their throat, we put a hallway's worth of distance between us in an instant.

Danny, Luna, and Nigel were watching us.

"Don't let Judith catch you like that," Danny teased.

Right. Sonya and I joined them and the five of us walked toward the parking lot.

Luna singing, "*Sonya and Jeremy sitting in a tree,*" should be soft enough no one but our group would hear her. Danny joined in.

Because of course he did. Not that I ever complained about hearing Danny sing—dude had a haunting baritone—but this was likely to draw attention.

When Nigel picked up the tune too, I almost

passed out from shock. Fortunately, no one else seemed to care what the five of us were doing.

When we reached our cars, Danny, Nigel, and Luna went their separate ways. I stopped next to Sonya's car, and she nudged me playfully with her shoulder. "You should still come back to my place."

Her whisper combined with a fried brain were enough to shove any negative thoughts out of my mind. I followed her home, letting my thoughts trip along half a dozen next steps once we arrived.

I parked in front of her house, met her in the driveway, and rested my hands on the roof of her car, on either side of her head, boxing her in.

"I can't believe they spent almost an hour arguing about condoms, after telling you we couldn't play Rule 34." Her face was pink from the cold, and illuminated by street lights. She looked positively angelic and completely delicious.

I dragged my nose up the side of her neck, inhaling her sweet scent. "We could make up our own Rule 34 right now."

"Porn of us?"

"Precisely." I nipped at her earlobe and slid a hand under her shirt.

She squealed when my cold fingers met her warm skin, but quickly relaxed against me. "What's the scenario?"

"Nothing elaborate." I teased my thumbs up her ribs, to brush the bottom of her breasts. "Best

171

friends and co-workers who want more out of their relationship."

"So they fuck on the hood of her car?"

I nipped at her lips. "Not unless they want ass frostbite."

"Now you sound practical, like Nigel." Sonya was playful.

"You take that back."

Sonya shifted her weight and her entire body rubbed against mine. "You know what makes most porn better?"

"Cheesy music and people actually enjoying themselves?" And this change back to the original topic.

"Well, you're not wrong…" She caught her bottom lip between her teeth.

I brushed my thumbs over her bra, teasing her nipples underneath. "What were you going to say?"

"An extra dick."

Should I be hurt or intrigued? I was too tired and turned on to know. "Well, you're not wrong…"

She nudged me back, grasped my fingers, and tugged me toward the front door. After a moment of fumbling, she fit the key in the lock, and let us inside.

"…yes, I made that." Quentin's voice drifted from the living room to greet us.

I was definitely intrigued. Extra dick it was. But who was he talking to?

"I wish she wouldn't flaunt that trashy game," Mary Russel's voice sent ice spilling through my veins and killed any arousal I had.

Sonya frowned and dropped my hand. "Hey, I guess my mom's here." Her voice was subdued.

19 /
sonya

Tension ratcheted through me at the sound of my mom's voice, and I was instantly both more exhausted and wider awake. Sometimes visits with her were great, and other times they were a subtle reminder that I didn't live up to her expectations—I wasn't the daughter she could parade in front of her friends and brag about.

But Jeremy being around tended to make things a billion times worse. He didn't like her.

Above all else though, she was still my mother. I squeezed his fingers and dropped his hand. "You should probably go home."

"No."

I didn't want to do this. I'd rather have his company, and that he and she got along, and that this night end on an up note. "Please. You're going to be miserable if you stay."

"Sonya—"

"Please." I didn't want to beg. I didn't want him to go. I needed him to.

"Sonya, is that you?" Mom's voice floated closer.

I looked at Jeremy with pleading on my face and he stared back with a mixture of fury, hurt, and resignation.

"I thought I heard you." Mom joined us. "Jeremy, hi. Nice to see you."

"Thanks." His voice was tight. "I was just making sure Sonya got home safe. I need to go."

"You can stay for a while," Mom said.

He kept his attention focused on me. "I really can't." And with that he was gone.

"Hmm." Mom's tone was noncommittal as the door closed behind him. She pulled me into a tight hug. "I missed you."

Quentin stood behind her, expression unreadable.

I squeezed back. This would be fine. This was friendly, sweet mom. Besides, I had TV deals pending. I was a bestselling author. I was full of brag-potential. "Missed you too."

She pulled away and tugged me into my living room and Quentin followed. "Your boarder was telling me all about your life right now," she said.

"Did he?" I almost froze to the ground, but I forced my feet to keep moving. If she thought my books were trash, there was no way she'd approve of what I was doing with Quentin and Jeremy.

"Mhm." Mom settled onto my couch like she'd always been there. "Volunteering. Working hard. I'm so happy to see you doing well in management."

I took the seat across from her, and Quentin settled into the other recliner. This wasn't so bad. "I'm really enjoying the work," I said.

"And your name is out there. You're a big deal right now." Mom sipped what was probably water from one of the delicate glasses she'd sent me as a gift two Christmases ago that I didn't dare use or get rid of.

"How have you been?" I wanted to leave things about me in a place we were both happy with.

Even this time of night, she was made up and put together more than I was on my best days. Given my schedule this week, I was grungier than normal in my most comfortable jeans and sweat-shirt, with my hair in a ponytail, my mascara smudged, and my lipstick gone hours ago.

"Good." Mom's voice was pleasant. "Wonderful, even. Everyone at the office is excited to meet you and work with ideas that you created."

This wouldn't be so bad. I could probably breathe again. As long as she didn't freak out when I said something along the lines of *there are multiple offers on the table, and I haven't decided yet.* Fortunately, my lawyer told me not to talk about that, so I could take a page directly from her book. "Mhm."

"I've always known how very talented you are.

It's lovely to see that shining through. It's so amazing to brag to my friends that my little girl's name is on the best seller lists."

"I'm forty, Mom. Hardly a little girl."

What did Quentin think of all of this? He was being awfully quiet.

"I'm a mom, I have some privileges. Of course, when they ask about your books…" She sucked in a sharp breath.

Fuck. Here we went. "I haven't eaten yet tonight. Can I make you some dinner?"

"I'm fine. I grabbed food before I came over."

"Go grab some dinner. I'll keep Mary company," Quentin's tone was difficult to read.

Somehow that seemed like a worse idea than leaving Jeremy alone with her. "I'm good. I'll get something after you head out."

Mom sighed heavily. "It's just so hard on me. I want to brag about you to everyone, and when you sign with us, and we clean up your words, the world will know you're my daughter."

"Sonya's words don't need *cleaning up*." A growl rolled through Quentin's retort.

"You know what I mean." Mom waved a hand dismissively.

Quentin scooted forward to the edge of his chair. "I don't. Explain it to me."

Fuck.

Mom gave him her full attention, brows raised. "I'm not sure that's possible."

No. I wouldn't listen to her do this. Couldn't. I was used to the backhanded compliments and I knew she loved me regardless, but my friends didn't get it, and she could be cutting when she wanted to. "It's late and it's been a long week." I stood so abruptly my chair nearly toppled. "Could we pick this conversation up tomorrow or this weekend?"

"I'm fine, thank you." Mom stared at Quentin. "I'd like to hear your boarder explain to me what he's thinking."

"He's my friend, not *my boarder*." I clenched my jaw. "And I need some rest."

Quentin stood as well, and moved to my side. "Ms. Russel, I'd be happy to see you to the door."

"I suppose I should be going." Mom took her time setting her glass on a coaster and smoothing out her clothing as she rose. She picked away a few pieces of invisible lint. "I'll call you tomorrow, Sonya. We'll have lunch."

Quentin moved between us and took a step toward her. "She has work tomorrow."

"They have to let you eat, don't they? You are the boss." She turned away. "I'll call you." She gave me another quick hug, passed a look of disdain to Quentin, and strode from the house without waiting for either of us.

I sank back into my chair with a heavy sigh. On

a scale of One to Five, Five being our best visit ever and One being our worst, this was a solid Three. Thank Goddess for that.

Quentin crouched in front of me and took my hand in his.

I couldn't deal with whatever he was about to say. Anger, sympathy, pity—I didn't want any of it. "How was your day?"

"Come with me." Command cut through his words and he tugged me to my feet.

I was too drained to argue, and I let him lead me into the kitchen. He sat me on a stool at the bar running along one side of the island in the middle of the room.

"I'll tell you, but you have to eat, too." Quentin was already going through the cupboards and fridge.

"You're a master negotiator, did anyone ever tell you that?"

He set a can of soda and a glass in front of me, followed by a plastic storage container and a fork. He popped the lid off the container, revealing left-over pasta salad which he must've made at some point during the week. "Never in those words. Pretty sure I've been called a bossy asshole, though."

"Pft. Whoever said that didn't appreciate you enough." When the words passed my lips, he raised an eyebrow. Was this where the retorts about my mom would start?

He shrugged. "I guess they didn't. Eat."

"Yes, sir." I put a forkful of pasta drenched in the yummiest sauce ever into my mouth. My stomach grumbled in response and I shoveled in more food.

Quentin leaned against the counter by the sink, facing me, his stance casual. "My day was... interesting."

"How so?" I managed between bites of food. I needed to sate the hunger and dull the edge of my mother's visit and unwind enough to sleep tonight.

"I met with Mick."

I almost choked on my food.

Quentin waited until I'd stopped coughing.

"How'd that go?" I finally managed.

"I don't know. I was furious at first, but he apologized, and he sounded sincere this time. What if he meant it?"

Something clenched in my chest, and I paused in my eating. Was I about to lose Quentin? Or worse, see him destroyed again? "Oh?"

"He didn't want to get back together or anything. I thought it would hurt to hear him say that, but it didn't. That's part of what I've been thinking about. He just wanted to apologize and explain."

"So... are you friends now?" I didn't have the mental capacity to process this on top of everything else, but worrying about Quentin was more important than whatever petty things I had going on.

"No. I walked out."

"Oh." Words were hard. "I might have some good news." Goddess, I hoped he saw it as good news. "Jeremy has an old garage on his property—it used to be a carriage house, but he doesn't use it for anything—and he was wondering if you could use it for a new workshop."

Quentin frowned.

"You don't have to. And it's not charity. And he's really not using it for anything so you wouldn't be intruding. And…" I let out a noisy exhale. "I don't know."

Quentin pushed away from the counter and moved closer. "It's a kind offer, and good news. I'll have to think about how I can use it. Thank you."

"You're welcome." I felt like a child out of my depth—the realization hit me hard, and suddenly I wasn't hungry anymore. I shouldn't. Quentin and I talked all the time. I was a fucking adult with a good life and career that I'd earned. Why did I want to wither and hide from it all, until I felt like I was good enough to be in my own shoes again?

"I grew up in a traditional, religious household." Quentin's statement came out of nowhere.

It wasn't about me, which made it easier to listen to.

He sat on the stool next to me and rested his

forearms on the bar, his shoulder pressing into mine. "My father was the man of the house, my mother was a homemaker, and we were always in the third pew from the front at church. Every fucking Sunday."

I couldn't imagine, but I'd never talked to Quentin about his past and I wanted to hear more.

"I tried so hard to be my father's son. Baseball, track, whatever he did or wanted me to do, I was there. But I also wanted to be in my room reading about dragons and spaceships. I wanted my mom to teach me to cook."

"Variety is good. Keeps the brain sharp." It was tempting to lean in closer and rest my head on his shoulder, but that was an impulse I shouldn't indulge.

He chuckled. "It's true, it does. I was never quite good enough at the things that mattered to him—I *suck* at baseball. I'd rather only run if a monster is chasing me. And when I was seventeen, and my father caught me kissing my best friend…" Quentin clenched his fist.

I covered his hand with mine, and he relaxed under my touch.

He breathed in through his nose. "He said some horrible things, the least of which was threatening to disown me. I had to prove to him I was still his son, so I enlisted. Nothing's more manly than being a Marine, right?"

"I'm sorry." That hardly seemed like an adequate response.

"It's okay. I've dealt with it now, but back then… I excelled after I enlisted. Promotions. Top marks. Straight track to becoming an NCO. When I was on leave my father would show me off to all his friends. I resented that this was what it took to earn his recognition and at the same time I felt like I'd finally found a place I belonged. It was a confusing time."

Quentin turned his hand so our palms were pressed together, and tangled his fingers with mine. Which one of us was holding the other?

"It took some time, and…" He closed his eyes.

I squeezed his hand.

He shook his head. "And then I met Mick. And he helped me figure out I needed my successes to be for me, not for someone else. That I was my own person—I wasn't my father's trophy."

His words cut deep, which he had to know they would after meeting my mom.

"She doesn't hate me. She just wants what she thinks is best for me." Or for her.

Quentin leaned his head against mine. "Your situation isn't mine. Do what *you* think is best for you, and regardless of what that is, I'm still your friend."

"Thank you for that." I was grateful to have him as a friend, and there shouldn't be any part of me that wanted more. He belonged with Jeremy.

Yet, I was glad I was the one here right now. It wasn't selfish to hold onto this for tonight, was it?

"What do you want to do tonight?" Quentin asked.

"Anything that doesn't require me to think." About *anything*.

"I have the perfect solution. *Supernatural* marathon until we fall asleep."

I grinned. "You say the sexiest things."

Quentin cleaned up quickly from my impromptu meal, then led me into my bedroom. "If you're going to fall asleep, we have to get ready for bed."

The puzzled look I gave him faded to surprise when he undid my jeans. He pushed those to the floor and stripped off my sweatshirt. Then he pulled one of my oversized shirts over my head.

If I felt small and lost before, this was a hundred times more potent. But so was the feeling of *safe* that came with it.

Quentin shed his jeans as well, turned down the blankets, and nudged me into bed. He curled around me, blocking out the rest of the world.

The TV played in the background, but I didn't give it much attention. All I wanted was to lose myself in Quentin and this sense of security for the brief time that I had it.

When sunlight hit my face through open blinds,

panic kicked in before the rest of my mind caught up.

It was February. If I was seeing sunlight…

I shot out of bed, adrenaline coursing through my veins.

"What's wrong?" Quentin looked drowsy and perfect lying in my bed.

"I'm late. *So* late." It was almost ten, and I was supposed to be to work before seven. "Shit."

He was up in an instant too. "What can I do?"

"I don't know. Nothing. I need to go." As I talked I yanked on some clothes. I ran a brush through my hair, slipped on some shoes, and was out the door in under ten minutes.

As I drove to the office, I let my phone play back the series of text messages waiting for me. From Judith. Luna. Jeremy. All asking where I was and if I was all right.

"*Fuck.*" I screamed in my car.

20 /
quentin

I hated seeing Sonya wake up in a panic and not being able to help beyond staying out of her way. There were some things I couldn't play the guard dog against and being late for work was one of them.

I couldn't believe I'd told her the story of my past last night, but I was glad I'd had the chance. No one but Mick knew that story before now. Back before he was the enemy. Back when it was okay to fall. Okay to trust.

Did I really regret my past with him?

No. The answer surprised me. I hated what happened to us and the way he left and the mess I was still recovering from. But I didn't regret what we had before then.

When I glanced at my phone to see a missed call from one of the temp agencies who sometimes had work for me, my heart dropped. They'd called almost three hours ago—there was no way the job was still available. Still, I had to call them back, just in case.

I started the coffee maker while I waited on hold. I gave the man who answered the phone my information. I waited a little more.

"Quentin. Oh my gosh, hi. Thank you for calling me back." Diane sounded like she was out of breath. "Your information says you can do tile. Tell me you're comfortable doing tile unsupervised."

"I can lay tile, no problem." Easiest question I'd had to answer in days.

"Oh good. Yay. I have a place that needs someone, and one of the two guys we sent over this morning was just... He lied about what he was capable of. Can you get there in the next half hour?"

Work would be wonderful. A little extra cash plus something to occupy my mind. "As long as it's in the valley, yes."

"Amazing. You're amazing." She gave me the address, promised to email it as well, and said she'd call the contractor and tell him I was on my way.

The site was about fifteen minutes away. An office building with a massive interior remodel, and the contractor was having trouble finding and keeping people. After about thirty seconds of rapid-fire questions around how I felt was the best way to lay tile, he pointed me in a direction. "Other guy is already in there. He's got all the information you need."

I headed to the room in question, one that was meant to be an on-site kitchen when we were done, and stalled in the doorway when I saw Mick in the far corner, on his hands and knees.

"Oh." The surprise escaped me before I could stop it.

He glanced over his shoulder, gave me a said smile, then nodded at the supplies. "At least they found someone who knows their shit."

My thought as well. I joined him, and we worked in silence. As much as I'd hoped this would be a respite from my thoughts, the conversation with Sonya kept bouncing in my head. Every bit of it, including the offer to use Jeremy's empty garage as a place to work.

I'd enjoyed the time spent in Brooke's workshop, and this was nice too, though I'd love the ability to improvise. Did I dare hope I could get back into something to do with welding?

Not without equipment.

"Is there anything left?" I asked Mick. "Any tools? Any gear at all?"

He glanced at me, then went back to his work. "Nothing worth mentioning."

"Mention it anyway."

"I still have the tools from when we first started.

Those ancient, underpowered things we used for our very first jobs."

Hope flitted in my chest. "Why?"

"They're not worth anything at a pawn shop." There was a hitch in his voice.

"But you didn't throw them out."

He shrugged and moved to the next section of floor to spread the mortar. "Sentimental value. They remind me of starting with nothing and becoming something."

I followed the path he created, laying down the membrane. "So you wouldn't be willing to part with them?"

"If you need them, they're yours. Not for anyone else, but for you, yes."

"Thank you." I knew which tools he was talking about and they really were old and shitty, but if they still worked, I could use them.

While I finished my step, Mick moved onto the next one, sealing the seams in the layer I'd put down. This didn't need any discussion. We'd always had a good rhythm working together, and that didn't seem to have changed.

"This woman you're living with—Sonya."

I was instantly on my guard. "Yes?"

"She's a girlfriend? A roommate?" Mick was gay, but he'd never questioned my bisexuality.

I hesitated. My answer should be easy—it never changed—she was a woman I rented a room from.

A friend of a friend. I didn't want to force out my reply. "I rent a room from her," I finally said.

"You sure? Because I know you, and—"

"You don't. Not anymore."

Mick nodded. "That's fair. But some things don't change. I can't imagine you've stopped being the loyal, loving, protective man who would do anything for friends."

"I hide it a lot better now." I couldn't keep the bitterness from my reply.

"I'm sorry."

"So you've said." I wanted to know if he was looking for more information about Sonya, but I didn't want to tip my hand about how much I cared. And I did. More than I wanted to admit even to myself. Thinking the words came with an ache. I cared a lot about Sonya and even Jeremy.

"Someone mentioned her in therapy the other day." Mick's casual comment and tone made my blood run cold.

"*Her* as in Sonya?"

"It's not whatever you're thinking, though," Mick said quickly.

I was thinking I might have to hurt someone if they came anywhere near her. "What am I thinking?"

"Something that requires you to be her guard dog."

"You're dragging this out a lot if that's not the

case."

Mick let out a short, dry laugh. "We were doing an exercise in the group where we envision good things happening to us. There are no restrictions. It's supposed to help us accept that we're allowed to have dreams and goals, even though we've screwed up."

I didn't like the sound of *no restrictions*, especially if some random guy was fantasizing and Sonya was involved. I let Mick kept talking, but my entire body was on high alert.

"This guy was a big name in Hollywood a few years back," Mick said. "Worked for one of the production studios, gambled a lot of money that wasn't his, and lost it all. He was saying his dream is to find that perfect diamond in the rough. That thing that people don't know they want, and make it into something spectacular that puts him back in the spotlight."

Sonya was stunning, but I couldn't imagine her being happy as an actor. Besides, how would this guy know her, to pick her out of every person in the world to say that about?"

Mick knelt, hands on his knees. "He basically said *like that author who came out of nowhere and became an overnight sensation. The one who topped the best seller charts literally overnight.*" Mick sighed. "He said if he could sign a deal like that, take the Hollywood bullshit out of the entire thing and let her be herself, bring the show to life in a way that her readers love, that a win like that could make him someone again."

I gave a dry chuckle. "Everyone always wants something." But it was better than some creeper fantasizing about Sonya.

We finished the layer we were working on, and set about marking the floor for the tiles.

"I have a hard time arguing with his dream," I said as we started to dry fit the tiles. "I'd love to see her have that."

"Loyal and protective for the ones you care about." There was a hint of longing in Mick's tone. "I could give him your name. See if there was any chance of making it happen."

"I don't speak for Sonya. You can give him her lawyer's name."

"Really? That would be incredible for him." Mick grinned. "You know, one of the things I loved about you back then was the way you looked at me. The way you looked when you talked to other people about me. That's gone. The resentment that's there now hurts, but I get it."

I was willing to give him more leeway than yesterday. Things didn't ache as much as they used to. "You helped me a lot when I was younger. I did love you for that and I haven't forgotten it. I hope to God you can find your way back to your own life, but I won't be a part of it."

"I know you won't, but thank you. I told you yesterday this isn't about winning you back."

"But?" I heard the *but* in there.

He put down spacers between the tiles I set on the floor. "But even if I wanted to, I wouldn't have a chance. The way you look when you talk about Sonya? That's the way you used to look for me."

I didn't know what to say. His comment sat in my head as we worked in silence again. Could I let someone into my heart the way I had with Mick?

I didn't know. Considering it hurt, but ignoring the hope hurt just as much.

21 /
sonya

When I got to the office, I was greeted with Jeremy's concern and Luna's, plus Judith's *I'm just glad you're safe* accompanied by a stern look of *I'm disappointed in you. You promised*. She didn't have to say it, I was repeating it in my head. The team had been counting on me to pull my weight, and I'd let them down.

The testing was done, though. It had wrapped up before I arrived, and the noise level in the office was decibels higher than normal, thanks to an entire staff doing nothing after almost a week of frying their brains.

I felt like I should still be working regardless. Like I hadn't earned the celebration the way they did.

"You put in as many hours as any of us the rest of the week." Jeremy put himself between me and my computer. "It's okay, really. Were things that bad last night?" *With your mother*.

I didn't need to hear the rest of his question to know it was there. "It could've been better. It also could've been worse. But I talked to Quentin after, and that helped a lot."

Jeremy clenched his jaw. "I'm glad he was there for you."

He was jealous. Because he wanted Quentin. I couldn't keep pretending I belonged with them or between them. It would hurt that much more when I needed to go back to anything but friendship with them.

"I'm here for you too. Always." Jeremy squeezed my shoulder.

"I know."

"Do you?" he asked.

How was I supposed to respond?

The ringing of my phone saved me from figuring it out. It was Dom. "Hello?" I switched to my phone voice in a blink.

"Sonya, hey. Do you have a moment?"

"Sure."

"I hate to do this, but I feel like it's always best to deliver bad news over the phone or in person."

My gut sank. "What bad news?"

"Three of the studios have withdrawn their offers. Only Epithet's remains."

Oh. "I see."

"I'm sorry. But when more call, make sure to point them in my direction," he said.

Like that was going to happen. The fervor had died in the last week, and like Mom had predicted, I was already fading into the background. "I will. Thank you."

So this was it. My fifteen minutes of fame were about to be over.

"Are you all right?" Jeremy asked. "What was that?"

I told him, barely holding back the tears of disappointment that clawed at my throat and my eyes.

He pulled me into a hug and held me. "I'm sorry." His voice was soft.

"Me too."

We sat there for a few minutes, and I let myself absorb as much comfort as I could.

"Hey, a bunch of us— Oh." Luna's voice came from behind. "I'll come back."

I dragged in a shaky breath and steeled myself. "It's okay. I'm okay. Just dealing with some news."

"We're going to lunch. Food makes a lot of things better," Luna said. "So does talking."

"You guys go, I'm good."

Jeremy studied my face. "Come on."

"Just give me some time. You can tell them why, I don't care."

He squeezed my hand. "We'll text you the address if you change your mind." His eyes grew wide.

Before I could ask why, I was almost knocked over from behind by Luna hugging me tight. "I hope you change your mind," she said, and left.

Jeremy forced my gaze to his. "I need you to remember something."

"What's that?"

"You're the reason you're at this point in your life. Your book hit bestseller lists because of you. It went viral on BookBocker because of you. Because of your talent, skill, drive. Your heart. You're not here because of anyone else, including your mother. *You* did this."

The words bolstered me in a way I didn't expect. They didn't cut through the disappointment, but they washed away a layer of self-doubt.

He kissed me on the forehead. "See you when I get back."

"Yeah." I shooed him out of the office and sank into my chair, letting disappointment wash over me. Why all of the sudden? It didn't make sense. Maybe one studio pulling out, but all three in one morning?

My phone rang again, and my mother's name flashed on the screen.

"Hi, Mom."

"Hi, Sweetie. I have an appointment with your

attorney in fifteen minutes. Would you like to join me?"

She wouldn't. She couldn't. Did she have the kind of pull it would take to get people to cancel contract offers?

No. "Very much so. I'll see you there."

I tried not to jump to conclusions as I drove the few blocks to meet her. Fifteen minutes. I was being manipulated into this. Why was she doing this to me?

Like last time I was here, we were shown to a conference room and Dominic was with us right away. Introductions and pleasantries were passed around, and I fluctuated between anger and doubt.

"This kind of meeting is atypical, especially so early in negotiations, but it's not unheard of," Dominic said.

My mom smiled her frustratingly professional smile that always played in my head with the words *bless your heart.* "I suppose *atypical* depends on how many of these you've been a part of. They're every day in my world."

I didn't miss the underlying hint of condescension in her words, and I hid my wince.

"I'm sure they are." Dominic remained stoic. "I suspect there are a lot of ways in which you conduct business differently than I do."

"Yes. I like to accomplish something with my work."

That time my cringe slipped out.

"I can appreciate that." Dominic sounded like he was discussing weather. "The details of the goals matter to me as much as checking generic items off a list. Let's get down to this. Are you certain you don't want your legal team on the line?" He reached for the speaker phone in the center of the conference table.

Mom shook her head. "That won't be necessary. They'll review the final contract before Sonya signs it."

"As I'm sure they do in your world, the words used mean everything in my line of work. *If* Sonya signs it."

And here I was a little girl again. Needing someone to fight my battles for me. It was so obvious to see what Mom was trying to do when I watched her talking to someone else, but when she directed it at me, I got lost in the words.

"The revisions you submitted to us include modifying rights reversion to specifically define *out of print* as physical copies," Mom said. "You do understand that most of these shows are only ever distributed electronically."

Dominic didn't so much as twitch a finger. "I do. Do you? It's not too late to loop in your legal team if you're concerned about following some of the more specific language."

I swallowed a smirk as my mom's jaw tightened.

The next fifty minutes or so were a lot of the same. I heard every subtle insult from my mom, an attempt to break down Dom's defenses, and watched in awe every time he reflected it.

Mom was mid-sentence, talking again about rights reversion, when Dominic looked at his watch and said, "I need to cut this short." He talked over her. "I have another meeting and I'm conscious how I spend my time when I'm billing clients."

"I'd just like to cover—"

"Which we've already done. Ad nauseam," Dominic said. "I'll have someone send a revised copy of the contract from today's meeting to your legal team."

We hadn't made any changes based on my mom's input. The document was exactly the same as what he'd submitted to her company already, unless I'd missed something.

Mom worked her jaw, then stood, smoothed out her trousers, and shook Dominic's hand. "I'd like to say it was a pleasure meeting with you today, but it wasn't. I'll ensure I note that to colleagues going forward."

I'd never heard anyone say *I'll tell my friends you suck* in such an elegant way before.

"I hope you do that." Dominic's smile was warm. "Enjoy the rest of your day." As we turned to leave, he called my name. "Will you stay for a moment?"

Mom sighed. "We need to go. I have a flight to catch."

Interesting how that wasn't a priority until just this moment."

"I'll have Reception call you a car for the airport if you'd like," Dominic said.

"I have it covered." Mom was already walking out of the office.

I hung back and closed the door behind her. It was a tiny thing, but it felt like defiance and it felt fucking incredible. I turned to Dominic.

His mask had vanished, replaced with a tired smile. "I understand how people feel about family—mine means the world to me."

Defensiveness rose inside. I'd had variations on the *your mom doesn't treat you right* argument with Jeremy too many times to not expect it. I didn't know if I could argue anymore, though.

"You hired me to do a job, so this is professional not personal. Please believe me when I say that." He sounded sincere. The cold, calculating tone from earlier was gone.

I wasn't prepared for anything that came next. "Okay?"

"Do not accept her contract. Don't continue negotiations with them. Walk away from this deal now. My advice has nothing to do with Mary's relation to you, but this is a bad deal and it will never end in your favor."

Talk about cutting straight to the point. I wanted to argue, but I also knew he was right. There was one thing he hadn't mentioned though. "The other offers are gone. What if I don't get any more?" It hurt far more to speak the fear than it had to think it.

"I've seen a lot of contracts over the years, and I've never seen an instance where a shitty one is better than none at all. If you want to continue negotiations with Epithet Romance, I will represent you, and I'll make sure you get the best deal they're willing to give. But you should expect that their stopping point will fall short of the point where I'd advise you to sign."

"I need to think about it."

"I understand. Call me with questions."

I thanked him. When I reached the lobby of the law offices, Reception told me that my mother was already downstairs. I found her on the sidewalk, looking between her phone and her street.

She smiled warmly as soon as she saw me, and I was instantly on edge.

"Sweetie, I'm sorry I couldn't visit longer."

"Mhm." I couldn't agree but I also couldn't make myself disagree.

She sighed and looked at me with a pity I'd come to expect from her over the years. "Before I go, I need to tell you something. I know you want to fly your own colors, and I understand that. You don't think I do, but I do. I'm so proud of you for being yourself and creating the art you want to create."

I grasped the nugget of praise harder and tighter than it deserved.

"But this isn't about the book of your heart, it's a commercial business decision. Your stories are not as commercial as they could be." Like that, she snatched that glimmer of kindness away again. "I want to see you succeed and discover your full potential. Your lawyer is in this for the paycheck, but I care about you. I'm in this for your future. Our company makes billions selling women the life they want. You're offering the kind of naughtiness that's fun to occasionally dabble in, but it's not reality."

"But it is reality." I might not be able to take a stand for myself, but I couldn't let her trash the world around me with her own jaded perspective. "I have friends who have that kind of love."

"So do porn stars, Hon. Orgasms don't equal love."

I clenched my fists. "Porn stars are people like anyone else, and what my friends have is very real."

"And this is why you're still single." Her tone was disgustingly sugary. She climbed into the car that had just pulled up and shut the door before I could respond.

Fury spilled inside me as I stood in the middle of the sidewalk, foot traffic parting around me.

And I hated that it was muted by the voice asking if my mom was right about me not being worthy of being loved.

22 /
jeremy

I bowed out of lunch early. I was too worried about Sonya to get into the fun, but at least most everyone sent me back with their sympathy and encouragement for her landing more TV or movie offers.

They were all going home from there anyway. No one was coming back to work today.

When I got back to the office, she was pacing the length of the Writers' room, a scowl etched on her face.

I stopped in the doorway. "What's wrong?" Not that she needed to add more to the list, but the atmosphere in here was heavier than when I left.

"Meeting with Mom and Dominic." She didn't look up. "Pretty sure she's the reason the other offers were withdrawn."

I didn't realize I was growling until the sound reached my ears. "Where's she staying? I'm going to talk to her." Fuck that woman. Sonya deserved so much better. From anyone, but especially her own mother, and I was going to tell her so.

Sonya shook her head. "Supposedly she's catching a plane so she's probably at the airport. *Fuck*. She tried to make Dominic look like an idiot. She failed, but… She made me look like an idiot. I can't believe I never saw… Why?"

The anger in her voice melted to frustration and her last question shredded my heart.

"Dominic advised me to walk away from her offer." Now sadness mingled with Sonya's words.

I'd held my tongue for so long about her mother because Sonya insisted *she's family. She loves me.* But that wasn't going to last. "You hired him because he knows what he's talking about."

"But what if I don't get another offer. My books could be on TV. *My* books."

"They wouldn't be though." I grabbed her wrist and yanked her to a stop, forcing her to look at me. "Your name would be in the credits"—I assumed. I hoped.—"but they wouldn't be your books. I'm going to call her. I'm going to tell her exactly what I think of this bullshit."

Sonya frowned. "And you don't think she'll tell you in return what she thinks of you? She spent last night calling Quentin *boarder*. She said it with so much disdain. The number of times she tried to imply today that she thought Dominic was an incompetent idiot. That my stories were shit covered cubic zirconia?"

And now I was angry. "Which is why I'm going to rip her a new one."

"And she'll rip back." Her phone rang and she ignored it.

"Don't you want the closure of telling her how she's treating you?"

Sonya shook her head. "I want her to understand how she makes me feel. If telling her doesn't do that, it doesn't matter."

"You don't see, do you?" My phone chimed with a new text, but this conversation was important.

"See what?"

I grasped her fingers in mine, and held her gaze. "This isn't about her. About whether she understands or not. It's about what *you* need, and if that includes telling that woman you're worth far more than she'll ever be is on that list, then it needs to be done."

Sonya worked her jaw. "I'm not. Even if she's wrong about how she treats me, I'm not what you think I am."

"But you are."

Sonya sighed. "You should see who's trying to get a hold of you." She grabbed her phone.

Like that, she'd shut down. I wanted to push, but I needed her to hear me, and right now she wouldn't. I glanced at my phone. "It's Megan," I said at the same time Sonya did.

She looked up from her own phone. "Mine's a voicemail. She says I have to call her back right now."

"Mine is asking where you are."

Sonya dialed, and the ringing echoed through the speaker of her phone. The conversation about her mother wasn't over, but concern for my sister was more immediate.

"Sonya, thank God." Megan answered with panic in her voice.

"What's wrong? What's going on?" I asked. "Do you need help?"

Her nervous laugh was tinny. "Nothing like that. Sorry to worry you. I just need to talk to Sonya."

"You should probably tell both of us. He looks pretty concerned." Sonya's tone was lighter and calmer than it had been seconds ago.

"I'm not in trouble or anything, I just found out…" Megan sighed heavily. "I need you to cancel any plans you made for my bachelorette party in two weeks, and I was hoping you'd have enough time to get deposits back and such."

That wasn't right. "Why?"

"Because we have other plans. A work thing for him."

Him would be her fiancé. "Sonya's had this planned for you for months."

"And that's why I wanted to talk to her, not you," Megan said.

Sonya gave me a look that was half apology, half *I'll handle this*, pressed a button on her phone, and put the device to her ear. "Are you sure you want to cancel?... The deposits aren't an issue, this is *your* party... No, I get it... What are you doing tomorrow night?... Good. You're coming to my place... It's a surprise... Of course a good one, see you then." She hung up and set her phone on her desk. "I need your help."

"Anything."

"I'm going to throw her a party tomorrow instead, and you're going to help me plan it."

"You got it, boss." That was something I could do. "The offices are basically closed for the rest of the day, we should go back to your place and do this."

"Loop Quentin in?"

I couldn't tell if her voice was hopeful or just a little sad, or...

Probably both, given the circumstances. "Exactly." I'd expected jealousy this morning when she told me Quentin was there for her last night when she hadn't let me be. Instead I was glad someone was there, and specifically that it was him.

"And you're sure we can take off for the day? I kind of feel like I should make up missing time from this morning."

"You shouldn't." I grabbed her purse and phone and put both in her hands. "Meet me at your place." If she wanted this as a distraction, I could deliver. Especially for a good cause like making sure Megan had a good party.

I was bothered that she'd cancelled the original. Or rather, that her fiancé had. But Sonya looked excited about making this new plan. And in a few hours, when she'd had time to think and was in a better mood, we'd loop back to her telling her mother to go to Hell.

When we got to Sonya's, Quentin's car wasn't there. I was more disappointed than I expected.

Sonya and I dove into party plans, which didn't take long. It came down to making sure she picked up some alcohol, adult party favors, and hired a striper.

That was the disappointing part—after calls to the few places we could find that offered such a service, no one was available on such short notice.

"Is it weird that we're trying to hire a stripper for a party where half the women are in relationships?" Sonya asked.

"It's a little weirder you didn't ask that before you planned the strip club visit for the original party."

"Fair point." Sonya let out a short laugh.

It was the best sound I'd heard her make all day. How could I get her to laugh more?

A short while later, Quentin walked in the front door. "Is Jeremy here?"

"Hello," I called.

He walked into the living room with a takeout bag in hand. "Good thing I brought extra."

"Dinner?" Sonya sniffed the air. "Pork buns?"

"Of course. And everything else we like. I got a cash bonus from today's job and I wanted to splurge." Quentin set the bag on the coffee table and started laying out boxes.

Sonya vanished into the kitchen and returned quickly with plates and two forks. Quentin wielded chopsticks like they were an extension of his hand as we all dished out a bit of everything. The way they did little things without any conversation made it clear this was a regular occurrence for them, but I felt like I was a part of it. A piece that slid into place rather than marring the picture.

"Can I assume if you're both here, it was a good day?" Quentin asked.

Sonya's frown flitted in and my anger at her mother surged back.

He looked at her then me. "What happened?"

"I can tell him if it's easier," I offered.

Sonya shook her head. "It's okay. Not that there's much to tell. Three of the four TV offers for my book were withdrawn."

Hearing it again made me just as furious, especially suspecting her mother was behind it.

"Fucking idiots. Why?" Quentin's tone and expression matched my thoughts.

"I don't know." Sonya shoved a forkful of food in her mouth.

I assumed that meant she was done telling her story. This was unfair.

Quentin set his plate down. "I don't want to get your hopes up because this probably won't go anywhere, but just in case... There's at least one other person out there who's interested."

I hit a pepper in my chicken and the pain seared up my throat. I gasped through the burn and downed a glass and a half of soda before I could breathe again.

"Can't handle the heat?" Quentin looked amused.

"Any time any place," I retorted, my eyes still watering. "Except maybe this time or place, or any similar."

Sonya's laugh was back. Not as easy as before, but still a lovely sound. "How do you know that? About the person who's interested?"

"I worked with Mick on the job site today," Quentin said.

He'd spent the day with his ex and came home in a mood like this? The feeling that clenched my chest wasn't from the peppers, and I liked it even less. "How'd that go?"

"It was..." He let out a long exhale. "Cleansing?

He's got some old tools I can use for welding. I understand you may have a space for me to work."

"I do." I was glad Sonya had told him, and the idea of having him working close by was much better than the feeling that came from his previous news. "But what does that have to do with…?"

"I'm getting to that. So, he knows a guy—from his gambling addiction group therapy which is why I'm not sure how real this is— who's says he's a big name in Hollywood. Gabriel Groves I guess? Something like that. Anyway, he says he's interested so I passed along Dominic's phone number."

I hated to be skeptical—Sonya's books were incredible and other people should think so too, but a big name like that?

Sonya's smile matched my thoughts. It was sweet of Quentin to try to cheer her up, but this one didn't feel like a real lead.

"Like I said, I don't know if anything will come of it, but don't write it off just yet," Quentin said.

His words lodged in my thoughts, attaching themselves to more than just the subject at hand. This afternoon, this evening, it all felt right. Was I writing off this relationship because of the past?

No. This wasn't the same at all as what Quentin said. I wasn't discounting Sonya's friendship or Quentin's. I was doing the opposite and holding onto what I had with them. Trying to not fuck up what a great thing I had with them.

"Is this a mourning party?" Quentin asked.

"No." Sonya huffed a sigh-laugh. "I definitely don't need to be wallowing tonight. We're planning a last-minute bachelorette party for Megan. Speaking of, can I kick you out of the house for a few hours tomorrow night? Unless you're secretly a stripper and want to be the entertainment for the evening."

"I'm definitely not, but I do know a guy. We served together." Quentin already had his phone out.

A few minutes later, Sonya had her stripper for her party.

We finished eating and cleaned up. As we settled in again, Sonya ended up between Quentin and me on the couch. "You know," he shifted his weight so he was sideways, one arm draped over the back and his leg pressing into Sonya's thigh.

"I might consider a limited edition career in stripping for an intimate audience of one or two." He trailed a light touch up her arm, raising visible goosebumps.

Her lips parted in a silent sigh.

I liked where this was heading. I wasn't sure what I was feeling for either of them—I didn't dare use the *L* word, but the emotion that filled me when they were around was different than with anyone else, and it was thrilling and terrifying.

"I wouldn't mind a show like that. Or being part

of one." I brushed Sonya's hair from her face and hovered my mouth near her ear. "What do you think?" I whispered.

Sonya stood abruptly, and I hurried to catch my balance. Her brows were furrowed, deep lines marring her forehead. "I think casual sex isn't the solution to every problem."

What the…?

"Solution?" Quentin asked.

"Celebration. Planning. Stress. Good news. Bad news. Sex isn't a band aid or a bottle of champagne," she said.

I definitely didn't understand how we'd gotten here. "Sometimes it is."

"You aren't enjoying this?" Quentin's confusion mirrored mine.

Sonya jammed her hands in her pockets and turned her attention to her feet. "It was good. All of it was really good, but I don't want to do it anymore. I don't want to do casual sex."

"One more night for the road, all three of us?" I teased.

"I said *no*." The sharpness of her voice sliced the air.

Seriously. What just happened? "Okay. No more."

"I'm sorry." Sonya raked her fingers through her hair. "I think I'm going to call it a night. Thank you both for your help. With the party and what-not."

215

The fact that I couldn't figure out how we got from where we were to here was proof I had no idea what a good relationship was. It was probably better she put an end to things now, before I confused myself further.

So why did I feel like I was about to lose something huge?

23 /
quentin

The night was all but over after Sonya pushed us away. Not that I wanted to walk away. Even without sex I was enjoying their company, and I would've stayed up half the night talking to Sonya and Jeremy if that was the way things unfolded.

But she shut down, and talking around her wasn't working for me. Jeremy and I managed long enough for him to invite me over during Megan's party to see if his garage would fit my needs and to give me a place to hang out.

I expected innuendo in the offer, but there wasn't any. I couldn't be the only one considering what it would be like to take things further between him and me.

When Jeremy announced he should be on his way for the night, I was disappointed but understood. Sonya mumbled a sad *good night and I'm sorry* and slipped away to her room. It was like the energy in the house was out of balance and there was no way to restore it.

Saturday morning wasn't any better. Sonya didn't come out of her room until after ten, and when she did, her head was down and she wouldn't meet my gaze.

"Do you need any help this morning?" I hoped to draw her out. "Shopping? Cooking?"

She shook her head. "I'm okay. I've got it under control."

I couldn't argue that—she was so tightly controlled she'd locked herself down.

"Have fun at Jeremy's." She grabbed a cup of coffee and turned away.

This was bullshit. "Sonya."

She took a few more steps before pausing, but she didn't look at me.

"Did I do something wrong?"

"No. I'm fine. Really."

I'd rarely heard a more blatant lie. I stepped in her path, placed a finger under her chin, and raised her gaze to mine.

She stared back, her expression flat except for the red rimming her eyes. As I searched her face, her chin quivered and she tried to pull away.

I tightened my grip. "Talk to me."

"What do you want me to say?"

"Anything, as long as it's the truth." I wouldn't direct my frustration at her, but I'd need an outlet for it soon.

Sonya shook her head. "I don't have any answers besides the ones I've given you."

Did her voice just waver?

"So give me something else. Conversation. A comment on the weather. *Something*."

"It looks like it's going to be a chilly this morning with some nice sunshine later."

I let go of her and jammed my hands in my pockets so she wouldn't see my clench my fists.

"You don't have to do this." Sonya's voice was definitely not steady.

"Do what?"

"Try to fix this," she said. "It'll be okay. I'll be okay. I know what the three of us had, and I just need some time."

I wanted to say I didn't understand, because the niggling of a clue I had didn't add up.

"Don't worry about it." The longer she talked, the more certain she sounded. "You don't need to reassure me or try to find comforting words. In a few days I'll be fine and it'll be like it never happened. It was sex, and it was really good sex, but I knew I didn't mean more."

I heard the *I* instead of *it* in her reply. "That's not—"

"Seriously." Sonya cut me off before I could give her a denial I hadn't thought through. "Go hang out with Jeremy. Have fun. The two of you are incredible together; anyone can see that."

Wait. What?

"I need to get ready," she said, and vanished into her room.

I wanted to kick in her door and make her explain. Get her to fill in the thoughts behind everything she just said. This wasn't the same as when Mick had started shutting me out months before he left, but in some ways it felt worse. I trusted Sonya to not betray me the way he did—a terrifying thing to admit to myself—but what if she vanished from my life?

The thought hurt more than I expected, squeezing like a clamp around my heart.

I couldn't stay here this morning. I left her a note on the whiteboard on the fridge to call me if she needed anything, and I took off. When I got into my car, my frustration broke loose, spilling through my limbs and clawing at my throat.

"*Fuuuuuuuuck*," I screamed as I hammered the steering wheel with the sides of my fists.

As I drove to Jeremy's, the vague and exasperating conversation with Sonya replayed in my thoughts. It was as though the entire picture was there, but I couldn't connect the dots.

When I reached Jeremy's, I wasn't any closer to

answers or understanding. He answered the door quickly after I rang the bell, a frown on his face.

He stepped aside to let me in. "Did you talk to Sonya this morning?" He asked.

Not the best greeting, but at least it was one I understood. "There were words exchanged. I'm not sure I'd call it an actual conversation."

"She texted me about fifteen minutes ago."

Which was right after I left. "Oh?"

Jeremy showed me his phone.

Sonya: *I'm tired of trying to hint.*

Jeremy: *At what?*

Sonya: *You and Quentin belong together. I know you're both hurting from the past, but it's obvious.*

Suddenly more of what she'd said in the kitchen made more sense. "Fuck me."

"I think that's what she's pushing for," Jeremy said dryly.

"So she thinks we're one of her fictional couples?" My frustration surged again, blending to anger.

Jeremy gave me a flat smile. "If she's right, you're definitely John Watson."

"Bullshit. Because there's no way you're Holmes."

"No? I figured this twisted shit out."

"She sent you a text. She fucking told you. You didn't figure anything out, and this isn't a joke."

Jeremy scrubbed his face. "I know. I thought we

221

were… And then last night… And it turns out she was never—"

"Homey, I'm a gnome." Nigel's voice came from behind me as he walked through the front door. "Shit. Do you want me to come back in five so you can finish whatever this is?"

"No." I bit off the word.

Jeremy gestured toward the back yard. "I asked Nigel if he wanted to help. That probably squashes Sonya's mastermind scheme. Do you want to see the place?"

"Are you sure you don't want me to come back? I'd never intentionally disrupt one of Sonya's plans," Nigel said.

"We're fine." Jeremy's tone conveyed we were very much *not*, and reminded me too much of my conversation with Sonya.

Nigel held up his hands, as if in surrender. "All right. *Fine* it is. Do you want to do this now?"

"Yes." *Doing* was exactly what I wanted.

Jeremy lived in one of the older parts of town, not quite at city center, but close, in a house on about an acre of land. A driveway led to a detached garage that was much newer than the house, and that same path kept going to a second structure in the back yard that was built from the same brick as his home.

Small windows ran along the top of the older building, near the roof. He opened a side door and flipped a light switch. Two rows of fluorescents flickered on above our heads, and kept flickering, illuminating a lot of dirt and leaves and a wall full of tools that were as much rust as metal.

"You didn't have time to lay down the plastic sheeting." Nigel's tone was a strained teasing.

I tried to chuckle. "I knew it. This is all part of an elaborate plan. To... kill me?"

"If bad puns and pop culture references are deadly, then definitely," Jeremy said.

What looked like minimal work at first turned into several hours of removing a layer of dirt, debris, and trash at a time. The three of us worked for several hours doing just that.

We were moving on to sweeping and scrubbing when Jeremy let out a soft *oh* and his hand dropped away from the portion of two-by-four he was de-griming.

Nigel glanced over Jeremy's shoulder, then frowned and turned back to his work. "She's in the past."

Curious. I couldn't help but look. It was a heart with J+J in the middle of it. Cliche, but also sweet. "Who's J?"

"Jeremy." Nigel's answer was less than helpful.

I rolled my eyes. "Thanks, genius. The other J?"

Nigel looked at Jeremy who shrugged.

"His ex-wife," Nigel said.

Ah. That made sense. I knew Jeremy had been

married, but no one had ever shared the details with me. "I'm sorry."

"It was what needed to happen. Sometimes the reminders just hit hard, you know?"

"I do." Especially after time spent with Mick this last week. I was curious, possibly more than curious if there was a level above that, but I wasn't up for prying, the way things had been going with Sonya.

We went back to work, the new silence in the room feeling heavier than the grime, and Jeremy moved away from the patch of wall in question.

"She was one of my best friends." Jeremy's comment came out of nowhere. "Worked with so many of us and the original crew at Cord and then Rinslet."

I didn't know how to respond to the statement. "Okay."

"So many of us had been working together for almost a decade. A lot of us had gotten married. Hell, some were already divorced." Jeremy's voice was more contemplative than sad. "A bunch of us were in Vegas for some show. Funny how I don't remember which one."

Nigel laughed. "There were a lot of Vegas shows. Pretty sure that was one with open bars in the courtesy suites."

"Definitely." Jeremy nodded. "We wouldn't have drunk that much if it was on our own dimes. But just like in the movies, drunk-Jenni and drunk-

Jeremy decided we were such amazing friends, we should get married."

"I'm guessing it didn't turn out like in the movies." I felt bad for Jeremy that he'd gone through such a thing. Was it weird that there was also a thread of relief that it hadn't worked out? That was fucked up.

Jeremy barked a laugh. "After a couple of years of what I thought was living with and fucking one of my best friends, she told me what we had wasn't love, and she wanted more out of life."

"Ouch."

"Yeah." Jeremy sucked in a sharp breath through his teeth. "I had no idea it was coming, I didn't understand at the time why she did it, and because we all had the same friends and worked with them, it pretty much tore the group apart. Everyone blamed me for pushing her away, especially when she quit and moved to another state."

"We didn't," Nigel said. "Yeah, there was some animosity when it first happened—Jenni was one of us and she was leaving—but that wasn't your fault, and no one thought that. She grew beyond us."

Jeremy's long sigh implied he wasn't sure he agreed. "One of the last things she said to me was that I was an immature man boy who would never recognize love."

"That was a decade ago."

I was with Nigel on this. "We were all immature man boys at thirty, and I'll tell you a secret about love." Wait. I didn't know any secrets. Did I?

"This oughta be good." Nigel leaned in.

It ought to be interesting, at least. "Everyone says you'll know it when you feel it. I call bullshit. Or rather, it's not nearly that simple. Love isn't enough. Sometimes it doesn't last. But everyone spends so much time searching for that elusive light-bulb that says *this person will be yours forever* that they miss out on the good stuff."

"Does that include you?" Jeremy asked.

Missing out on the good stuff in my never-ending quest for a love that was guaranteed to not hurt? "I think it might."

"I like this guy." Nigel turned back to his work. "Smart *and* pretty. He'd be perfect for—"

Jeremy smacked him on the arm.

"Sorry," Nigel said.

I was so tired of incomplete thoughts. "Perfect for what?"

Nigel grabbed his phone from his back pocket. "Look at the time. Wow, it's late. I should go."

"It's three in the afternoon." No, really. I was sick of this.

Nigel wiped his hands on one of the cleaner rags we had for things like that. "It'll be dark in less than three hours. I hate driving in the dark. Catch you Monday, Jeremy. Great hanging with you,

Quentin." He backed out of the shed like his ass was on fire.

"Few things have ever been less subtle," I said.

Jeremy leaned against the nearest support post, arms crossed. "He was going to say you'd be perfect for me, if I hadn't been hung up on Sonya since I met her."

Wow. "You know that for certain."

"I do. She's not the only one who's tried to set me up over the years."

I processed the words. "So she's tried to push you toward someone else more than one."

"No. She hasn't. He has. She's got a better eye for chemistry between people." Jeremy looked at me.

It would be easy to just stare back. To gaze into his eyes and see what kind of answers sat there. I didn't appreciate Sonya matchmaking me, but she did have good taste. The thing was, I couldn't let her go. Like Nigel hadn't said… *If I wasn't so hung up on Sonya.*

"I think though, that if love is possible—if it's a real thing—then being able to love more than one person is possible, too." Jeremy kicked away from the wall and turned back to the heart with J+J in it. "Hand me the orbit sander."

I did, and listened to the device whir over wood as he erased the crudely carved mark from the interior wall. *Love* wasn't the right word for how I felt about Jeremy, but it didn't taste wrong, either. Could it become the right word? Did he think it already was?

He finished and set the tool down. "I don't think you and I are there yet, but would you really write off a chance to find out if we could be?"

"I really wouldn't."

24 /
sonya

I didn't want to be harsh with Jeremy and Quentin last night, and *Goddess* pushing them away hurt. But better now than a month or two down the line, when I was so addicted to what we were doing that I crumbled from losing it. If having those TV offers withdrawn to buy my rights almost crushed me, I didn't want to think about how I'd react to having to admit Jeremy and Quentin weren't mine long term.

I was happy being friends with them, and I couldn't risk losing that.

Unless I was being an idiot about the entire thing.

When I saw Quentin this morning, it had taken all of my restraint to not stay and talk. I wanted to sit and chat and see if he'd flirt and tell him I was wrong to cut him and Jeremy off the way I did last night.

To beg him to let me pretend things meant more than sex.

And that one thing was what made me keep my distance.

I could shove thoughts aside for more important things, as long as I was working. Fortunately, today was Make Things Awesome for Megan Day. I already had a plan for that and it had much better odds of turning out the way I envisioned than me moping over men who weren't mine.

I'd spent the morning shopping and the afternoon baking pigs in a blanket and sugar cookies shaped and frosted like gray sweatpants. By the time the first guests arrived, penis streamers hung on the walls and drinks and appetizers waited on the dining room table, like a buffet of I'm-going-to-be-so-sick-in-the-morning-and-I'm-not-going-to-regret-it.

Not everyone could make it with the last-minute schedule change, but in addition to Carly, Megan, and me, there were three other women. Gretch was one of Megan's best friends and her wedding planner. Evie was my kind of nerdy—an electrical engineer who owned a hardware store in a small town in the mountains. Zoey was a competition gamer and gaming streamer.

We started drinking and playing silly games right away.

Adult Pictionary quickly degenerated into

pictures of large dicks and boobs with stick figure arms and legs. It was funnier with a couple of shots of liquor in me.

I hadn't planned the timing well at all. The stripper wouldn't be here for an hour, and I didn't have any other games to play. Why hadn't we come up with more games last night when I was planning with Jeremy and Quentin?

Thinking their names sent a wave of sadness through me. How did I miss them already? It had been less than 24 hours since I last saw them, and it wasn't like they were gone from my life. I'd just vowed not to sleep with either of them anymore. I poured myself a shot of something green and vaguely licorice-smelling.

"We should play *Drink if…*," Megan said.

I was intrigued.

"What's that?" Gretch asked.

"It's like *Never Have I Ever,*" Carly explained. "Someone says an event, like sex in the back seat of a car or sex in a dressing room, and if you've ever done that thing, you have to take a drink."

I wasn't sure I liked the topic. Or rather, the reminders that came with it. "Do they all have to be about sex?"

"No." Megan shook her head more furiously than was needed. "Well throw some things in there for those of you who are boring, to make sure everyone gets drunk."

I stuck my tongue out at her and swallowed another shot. "That's because I've done one of those."

"We haven't started yet," Carly said.

I shrugged. "We have now."

"Fine. You pick next, then." Megan poured herself a shot and waited.

I should give them a chance to catch up. "Slept with someone who has the last name of Cocker." Easton's last name.

Megan, Gretch, and Evie took a drink. It was a good thing I'd hidden everyone's keys when they arrived and told them to plan on crashing here tonight. Though it wasn't such a good thing that I asked the stripper to come *after* the drinking games.

I'd have to remember that next time. Though, if I was lucky, I'd forget a whole hell of a lot tonight. Every time I let my mind settle, I remembered the last few weeks with Jeremy and Quentin. How good it felt to be with them. Not just the sex, but there was a closeness that had happened too.

I downed another shot.

"When did you go skydiving?" Carly asked.

Oh. Shit. "Um, in my dreams?" I tried to laugh off the mistake. "Maybe no more *Drink if...* tonight."

I needed to empty my head, and the noise and alcohol weren't doing what I wanted. The laughter was drilling into my thoughts, though. I adored all of these women, but there was a reason I skipped most parties. My people meter didn't hold very much.

If I took a few minutes to catch my breath, I'd be okay and then I could laugh with everyone else again. As the topic shifted to a new tangent, I slipped away to the kitchen.

I was standing by the sink, drinking in lungfuls of air and trying not to think about Quentin and Jeremy, when Megan joined me.

"Thank you for tonight. For all of it." Her cheeks were flushed and there was a faint slur to her words.

"Of course. Anything for you."

Megan leaned her head on my shoulder. "You're lucky."

I didn't feel it tonight. "For what?"

"You're a bestselling author. People love your words so much they build games around them and want to make TV shows out of them. You have two perfect guys—okay, one gorgeous guy and one cynical idiot—who worship you—"

"They don't." And now the thoughts of Jeremy and Quentin were back.

"They do. I wish I could… Never mind."

Something in my mind snapped. I hated seeing Easton treat Megan the way he did, and my filter was already clogged with an assortment of liquors.

"Why don't you leave him and find someone who's worthy of your loyalty?"

"Because he loves me." Megan's answer came out so tiny I barely heard it.

My heart cracked for her and my stomach lurched. "Does he?" I winced as soon as I asked the question, but I could tell from her hurt expression it was too late to take it back.

"You've been spending too much time with Jeremy." Now Megan sounded upset. "He's infected you with bitterness."

Might as well finish the conversation I started. "Easton treats you like shit. We love you and we all see it. I'm sorry."

Her chin quivered and she let out a huff. "I'm almost forty." Megan's voice cracked. "What if there's no one else who wants me?"

"In the whole wide world? I guarantee there are other people who want you. Even in this city." I softened my voice.

"But how do you know?"

"I write romance for a living. I know a wonderful, lovable heroine when I see one. Besides, isn't no relationship better than being in one where you're not treated like his equal?" I almost gagged on the words as they mingled with Dominic's from yesterday.

Megan huffed and leaned against the counter next to me. "You're drunk."

"So are you."

"Then we can take it all back in the morning."

I didn't want to do that. The only thing I wanted to do was take back pushing away—

The doorbell rang, slicing through my thoughts.

"*Stripper's here*," Carly called from the other room.

"Yay." Megan grabbed my hand and yanked me back toward the living room.

The man standing in my entry way was gorgeous. Short, blond hair, a wiry muscular frame, and camo pants and a T-shirt that were probably two sizes two small.

He reminded me of Quentin. Why was I here instead of spending time at Jeremy's with them?

I grabbed the closest beer, popped the top, and took a long swallow. The music wound up, and I played along with the whoops and cheers as Landon shimmied his way out of his clothes.

What was wrong with me that I couldn't get into this show? Even when he was stripped down to nothing but a thong, his erection obvious, my thoughts were somewhere else.

When he asked where the bride-to-be was, he shifted his attention to Megan. There was a lot of grinding and no protest. She looked cuter with him than Easton, but who was I to match people up?

He finished his dance, but didn't seem to be in a hurry to leave. Instead, he pulled on enough clothes to cover his dick, and let the women pull him onto the couch for conversation.

I wandered into the kitchen again, so many thoughts overlapping in my mind. Why was I giving advice to Megan when I couldn't even make smart decisions myself? Why had I pushed away amazing men? I really didn't know. The reasons I'd given were there, but I didn't believe them.

And why was I letting my mother walk all over me, after all these years?

I fumbled with my phone when I pulled it from my back pocket, but once I had it securely in hand, it was easy enough to dial her number.

I went straight to voicemail. That was fine. She could screen me or spend time with people she thought were more important than her own daughter.

When the beep sounded to leave my message, I hesitated.

That least beer had my back. "Hi, Mom. It's me. Your daughter. Remember? The ball of flesh and blood you popped out of your uterus forty years ago? Maybe you forgot when you hopped back on the plane. Whatever. It doesn't matter." The longer I talked, the faster the words flowed.

"You're mean. To everyone unless you want something. You're manipulative and cruel. I'm your fucking daughter and you treat me like a commodity rather than a person you raised. Do you even love me, or do you just love the idea of bragging rights? You tried to humiliate me in front of my lawyer. What's the fucking point of that? And Quentin isn't just my *boarder.* He means so much more to me than you'll ever understand and so does Jeremy and fuck you and your *that's not reality* because it's my reality and—"

A beep cut me off, and a mechanical voice said *Message sent.*

I wasn't done yet. I hung up and called right back. As soon as the voice mail picked up, I said, "And one more thing—take your lousy fucking rights offer and shove it up your tight twat with all the sand that's in there."

I disconnected, spun, and emptied the contents of my stomach into the sink.

25 /
jeremy

Quentin and I stood at the edge of the now-clean carriage house. The room needed paint, furniture, tools, and something to replace the almost-strobe-like effect from the existing lights, but it looked good in here. Like I was taking a new step in my life.

It wasn't that this specific building was tied to my memories of Jenni—the whole house was. But cleaning out this spot for Quentin was cleansing for me as well. It was a new beginning.

And *fuck* I wished Sonya was here to share this with us. At least Quentin was.

"What do you think?" I asked.

Quentin looked at me and smirked. "I think you have sawdust in your hair." He trailed his fingers through the strands, sending sparks of need racing over me. I wanted him to tighten his grip. To pull my hair, claim my mouth, and make me groan.

"It's not sawdust, it's man glitter." I grinned.

He snorted. "That makes it better?

"Absolutely not. It makes the entire thing far more ludicrous."

"That sounds more like what I'd expect."

The banter was fun, but I wouldn't be distracted. Yet. "You didn't answer my question."

He looked away with a sigh, sweeping his gaze over the room.

He was quiet so long I almost prompted him again.

"I think it feels more right than a lot of things have in a long time," he finally said.

Did he only mean the garage, or was there more to the thought? If I asked him to clarify, I might get an answer I didn't want to hear. I wanted a long-term romance with both Sonya and Quentin. The realization slammed into me at high impact and with a reality I couldn't deny.

He was here, so it was a great place to start, and I prayed to God she heard us out in the morning. I didn't know if Quentin was in, but every instinct told me he would be.

I pulled my keys from my pocket and twisted one free from the ring that I'd had made this morning. "I hope you get a lot of use out of the garage." I pressed the key into his palm. "Don't abuse that— it opens the doors to the house too. Use the place whenever you want."

"That means I could sneak into your house any time, and take advantage of you."

I liked the implication of that. "It absolutely does."

"That's a lot of power to give me."

"You don't have to wait."

Quentin studied me with what looked like uncertainty.

I could be more direct. "As in, you could take advantage of me right now."

"Be careful what you ask for…"

I leaned closer, my mouth near his ear. "You could pin me to the wall by the throat, kiss me until I couldn't breathe, and fuck my face, and I'd love every minute of it." I dropped my hand below his waist.

Quentin grabbed my wrist in a flash and pinned it above my head. "Sometimes you talk too much."

"Sometimes?"

"But most of the time, it's perfect." He crushed his mouth to mine.

Despite the chill in the air, the heat of his body pressed to mine kept the cold at bay. Quentin was edges and roughness, from the way his calloused fingers dug into my skin to the scrape of his stubble against my neck.

I lost track of time and everything but him as we explored each other over clothes and exposed skin with our mouths and hands. With each new touch, my cock grew harder, until I was pretty sure I could cut diamonds with it.

I kissed along the front of Quentin's shirt, and scraped his nipple through the fabric with my teeth. He sucked in a sharp breath through his teeth, and pressed his hand to my throat, holding me in place.

The way he bit at my bottom lip, I knew I was on the menu, and he finished with deep kiss I felt in my toes.

Quentin dropped his hand to stroke my erection through my jeans. His grip was rough, magnifying the friction from the denim until the pain hurt so good.

"I liked the feeling of your mouth on my cock the other day." His low voice made me want to whimper and submit. "I want that again."

I didn't need to hear that twice. I lowered myself to my knees, freed him, and teased my tongue along the head of his cock. The way he grunted with each lick was motivation for me to draw out the fun.

"Enough teasing." Quentin tightened his fingers in my hair and thrust into my mouth.

I sucked him, using the sounds he made to go faster or slower. To stroke him as well or to finger his sac. I wanted to take out my own cock and do both at the same time, but my hands were full. The cold stone bit through the knees of my jeans. The wind whistled outside.

I wanted him to come, though.

I was surprised when Quentin stopped me and urged me to my feet.

"Something wrong?" I asked.

His wicked smile threatened to consume me with anticipation. "I want more than this," he said. "You have lube inside?"

"I do."

He didn't bother to put his dick away as we headed inside. Not that it mattered—it was dark and cold outside and the instant we reached my bedroom, the two of us were a chaotic whir of limbs as we rushed to help each other out of our clothes.

I directed Quentin to the lube and condoms, and in return he pushed me onto the bed on my hands and knees. The cold was back with a shock when the lube touched my skin, but it warmed up quickly under Quentin's liberal ministration.

It had been a while since someone was inside me, and the anticipation cranked my pulse up until the noise hammered in my ears. He nudged my asshole with the head of his cock, and I groaned at the first stretch.

The way he inched inside me seemed to take an eternity, and then he was buried deep. He reached around to grip my shaft. The possession in his touch, falling at the end of the drawn out make-out session and blow-job in the garage, was almost enough to make me come.

He stroked me as he hammered inside me,

squeezing my cock until it hurt. Jerking me and slamming against me hard and fast.

Desire roared in my veins, building in surges, until my dick ached and my balls were tight with need. I tightened my fists on the sheets. Climax built and my breath came in short gasps for air and release.

I came hard in Quentin's fist, grunting with each squirt until I was spent and had to shove his hand away.

He moved both his hands to my hips, his grip slick, and it was as if he'd been taken off his leash. Each slam inside me was delicious. He let out a loud groan and shudder when he came.

The frenetic electricity in the room faded as he slowed to a stop. We collapsed on top of each other, lying there as Quentin softened and fell out of me.

It took a lot more effort than I wanted for us to get up long enough to clean up, and rather than waste time getting dressed, we rushed under the blankets and cuddled next to each other.

I lay with my head on Quentin's chest. This felt right in a way I didn't expect. Only one thing—or rather one person—was missing.

"Sleep-wise, you're welcome to the guest room tonight, but I'd rather have you in my bed," I said.

Quentin's chuckle rumbled through me. "It's eight at night, old man. You tired already?"

Not even close. "I'm not sure when I'm going to sleep again. And you need to know something."

"We just had a great day and a better evening. Are you sure you want to risk that with *knowing something*?"

I wasn't sure at all, but I didn't like keeping this to myself. "Tell me you're not tired of having answers."

"I'm so tired of it."

Here went nothing. "This isn't just friendship to me. Not anymore. Not with you and not with Sonya. I want long term from both of you." It was both terrifying and a relief to push the words out.

When Quentin gripped the back of my neck, comfort and desire flooded me. He pressed his forehead to mine. "I like the sound of that." His voice was rumbly and sexy. "I want the same."

I hoped Sonya did too, but this was incredible as its own thing.

26 /
quentin

Sunday morning I was torn between waking up Jeremy for a little more play or rushing home to Sonya. The choices were much better than most I'd had recently, but in the end I knew getting back to Sonya with Jeremy was the best option.

Until then, I settled for searching his kitchen enough to make coffee. While the life-giving juice was brewing, I replayed yesterday. Did it really happen the way I remembered?

I wouldn't admit it if asked, but I was scared. Of falling without a net. Of what came next. Of things going wrong.

Not that I thought they would go wrong. My experiences with Mick said I wasn't always a great judge of that, but I wasn't willing to pass up more time with Jeremy, with Sonya, out of fear.

I was pouring myself a cup of coffee when

Jeremy wandered into the room, so I made him one as well.

"Give a guy a key to your house and he makes himself at home." Jeremy's voice was sleepy but teasing.

I handed him a drink. "You knew I'd take advantage of you."

He took a long drink of scalding liquid, and I took the chance to admire the view. His fleece bottoms hung low on his hips and he hadn't put on a shirt. His frame was wired with the slightest hint of a gut I assumed would show more with age.

I looked forward to sticking around for that. The thought should feel strange and instead it was right.

Jeremy let out a groan and set his mug down. "You hurt me so good."

"Next time you have to beg," I teased.

"Gladly."

I wrapped an arm around his waist, trying the gesture out for fit. Especially when he draped his arms around my neck and molded his body to mine. This was intimate and perfect. I brushed my lips over Jeremy's and he leaned into the kiss,

"I could get used to this in the mornings," he said.

Me too, with one exception. "You don't think it's missing someone?"

"It definitely is." He kissed me again. "Do you want to go soon?"

I didn't want to pull away from this embrace. As simple as it was, it reached deeper inside me than any sex we'd had up to this point. At the same time, we were down a person, and Sonya was as important a part of the picture as Jeremy was.

"Yes." I forced myself to step back, and playfully slapped his ass. "Get dressed and we'll leave."

He drove and a short while later we were parking in Sonya's driveway. There were a few unfamiliar cars here as well, which didn't surprise me. Seeing Landon's car did.

When Jeremy and I stepped through the front door, a war zone greeted us. Maybe not quite, but I'd been in a few urban settings when I served and in a way this resembled them. Bottles and cups were strewn across the coffee table and floor, and bodies lay on furniture in the most uncomfortable looking positions.

Sonya was in one of the recliners with Carly.

I picked our way through the carnage while Jeremy followed, and gently shook Sonya awake.

Her eyelids fluttered open, then she scowled.

Not what I expected.

She blinked a few times, scrubbed her eyes, then looked at us again. Her expression softened. "Okay. There really are only two of you." She cringed and smacked her lips. "*Ugh*. What did I drink?"

"Little bit of everything," Carly muttered. "Get off me."

Sonya stumbled to her feet and I helped her steady herself.

Jeremy reached past me to hand both the women glasses of water. I hadn't even noticed him leaving.

Carly looked at me. "Oh my God, Quentin. I need to talk to you." Her drowsiness vanished.

Sonya cringed and covered her ears with her hands. "Not so loud."

Poor thing. "Talk away," I said to Carly. I'd rather be kicking everyone out so Jeremy and I could talk to Sonya, but hangover cures were in order first, and I couldn't be rude to their friends and family.

"That thing you made." Carly stood, wobbled, and caught herself on the back of the chair. She pointed to Sonya's mantle. "The game logo sculpture. Do you take commissions?"

"Yes. He does. He absolutely does." Like that Sonya sounded lucid.

I glanced at her and she stared back. "Don't you?" She asked.

"I do," I said.

"Okay, so picture this." Carly was far more alert than a moment ago. "The company I work for is investing in a chain of boutique theaters. It's the full-blown movie experience. Nice seating, actual food, alcohol. Like taking the best of movies at home and at the theater and putting them in the same place."

Which sounded cool, but it didn't have anything to do with me. "I'm not licensed. You'll need to talk to someone else."

"I know, I know. But he wants a centerpiece at each location. A one-of-a-kind sculpture," Carly said.

"He'll do it," Jeremy answered before I could.

I stared at him.

He shrugged. "Won't you?"

"I will. But I have one other project first. I promised Sonya I'd make something for Megan."

Sonya grinned. "You will? Yay." She clapped then winced. "Too loud."

"Where is Megan?" Jeremy looked around the room.

I did the same. The other women were getting up. Talking quietly with each other. Wishing Sonya a bleary-eyed goodbye. But Megan was nowhere to be seen.

"I don't know." Sonya frowned.

"Her car's outside." I didn't know if that was helpful or not.

Megan wasn't in the living room or kitchen. The half bath down the hall was open and no one was in there. In fact, the only door closed was the one to Sonya's bedroom.

Jeremy, Carly, and I stayed close as Sonya pushed into the room.

Megan and Landon were laying on Sonya's bed, fully clothed and wrapped up in each other.

"What the fuck?" I asked at the same time Jeremy did.

27 /
sonya

My head was pounding, my stomach churning. I had vague memories of a drunken call to my mother last night, and my best friend was in my bed with the stripper I'd hired for her bachelorette party. And Carly had just offered Quentin a job?

"Wake up, wake up, wake up, wake up," I muttered under my breath.

"Not a dream," Carly said dryly.

Fuck. Fuck. Fuck. Fuck. Fuck.

Megan and Landon looked horrified, while Jeremy and Quentin were furious.

Was Carly smiling?

"Nothing happened." Landon was on his feet and as far from any of us as possible in a heartbeat.

Megan pushed to the edge of the bed. "We were just talking. *God*, please don't tell Easton."

She was fully clothed and Landon was wearing a

lot more than he had been at most points last night. Story checked out to me.

"I swear to you." Landon looked at Quentin.

Jeremy smacked Quentin's arm lightly. "You could've warned me. She's my sister. She's engaged."

Quentin held up his hands. "Don't dump this on me. This is on them."

"You don't even want me to be engaged," Megan said. "Don't pretend that's part of the issue."

Carly was definitely laughing.

My phone rang from somewhere in the house. *Goddess* I needed to be back at a point in my life where I could leave that thing on *Vibrate*.

My head was throbbing. I couldn't do this. "Stop." I talked over everyone, and four gazes turned toward me. "Carly, take Megan home. I don't care whose. We'll drop off her car later. Landon, thank you for the last-minute entertainment." I winced at the words. "I guess... bye?"

"I promise I won't tell," Carly said as she tugged Megan to her feet and toward the front door.

Landon followed shortly after them.

When everyone was gone except Jeremy and Quentin, I sank onto the recliner again, and dropped my head into my hands.

Jeremy's light laugh reached my ears, then grew louder. Quentin joined in.

I dared peek out between my fingers to see them both with huge grins. It was enough to chase away some of the ringing in my ears. I tried out a smile and it didn't hurt so I let it stay. "Why are we laughing?"

They shared a look I didn't understand.

"Not sure if you had more fun than we did, but it's got to be a more interesting story," Jeremy said.

Quentin twisted his face. "I don't know that it has a better conclusion. It's got a lot more dick." He pointed at the banner. It had come down at some point in the night and now a strand of penises hung in the middle of the living room.

Jeremy shook his head. "I don't know about a *lot* more. It has a little more."

"How do you quantify that, really?" Quentin asked.

This was better than last night. Better even ten minutes ago. "I'm glad you're both here."

Jeremy knelt in front of me and grasped my hands between his. "We need to talk."

"And like that, I'm going to be sick again." No good conversation ever started that way.

He kissed my fingertips. "I promise it's not bad. Not even a little."

Then why didn't he just come out and say it?

My phone rang again, from the end table next to me. A glance at the screen showed *Mom* and her picture, and my nausea surged back.

"What's wrong?" Quentin asked.

The biggest thing? I hadn't drunk enough last night to forget what I'd done. "I may have left her a voicemail last night. Or two. Telling her off. Telling her to take her rights offer and fuck off."

Jeremy and Quentin were laughing again.

"It's not funny." I rubbed the throbbing spot in my forehead.

"Sorry." Jeremy almost sounded like he meant it. "Do you regret it?"

Did I? "I regret that she's about to get mad at me. But not the kind of screaming anger most people are when they get mad. This will be quiet and seething and cold." And I wasn't sure I was mentally up for her tearing me down.

"Hey." Jeremy was still crouched in front of me. He rested a hand on my cheek. "She's wrong. Anything she says is bullshit. You can't trust her and you know she's wrong."

"And if you falter, we'll remind you again and again. As long as it takes," Quentin said. "You don't have to talk to her now. We're here when you're ready."

I wanted to know what Jeremy was going to say, but I would be fixated on my mother's reaction to my calls until I spoke with her. I drew in several deep breaths to calm my stomach. "Let's get it out of the way." Time to answer my phone. "Hi, Mom."

"Hi, hon. Are you all right?"

Her casual tone cranked my tension rather than soothing me. "I'm fine."

"Are you sure? I got your messages last night and you sounded… off. Like you'd been drinking."

"I was." No reason to hide it. "But I meant what I said." Not as cruelly as I'd said it, but if I gave at all, she'd see it as a weakness.

Her heavy sigh drilled into me. "I know I haven't always been the best mother, but you were a difficult child."

I didn't realize I'd clenched my fist until Jeremy covered my hand with his. This was the way we were taking the conversation, huh? "I was the best child I could be. Especially under the circumstances."

"And you don't think it was the same for me?" Her voice quivered. "This has been a horrible week. Dragstrip is having tummy issues and the vet visits have been just awful." Dragstrip was her fucking dog. "He's the only baby I have without grandchildren. And then you tell me you won't work with me? I try so hard, Sonya. I don't know why you hate me."

"I don't hate you." The reassurance slipped out and I winced.

"It sounded like it."

"The point is, I'm going to take my book someplace else. You can't buy the rights."

Mom made a *tsk* sound. "You're making a big mistake."

"Then at least I did so because it was my decision."

"Give me the phone." Jeremy's low but firm voice caught my attention.

I shook my head.

He met my gaze. I had no idea what he was trying to convey, but I caved. I handed the phone over in the middle of my mother rambling about how irresponsible and immature I was being.

"Ms. Russel," Jeremy said. There was a long pause. "*Ms. Russel.* You have your answer... Her assistant... I don't know why she wouldn't have told you..."

I couldn't hear my mother's replies, but I heard the way her voice fluctuated between shrill and calm.

"Stop, please. You're embarrassing yourself," Jeremy said. "I don't give a fuck who you are to anyone else. You're no one to me. Sonya is at the center of my universe and I love her for her heart and mind. If you're incapable of doing the same..."

I barely heard anything else he said, because Jeremy's *I love her* was ringing in my ears.

"Sonya will call you if she needs to speak with you. Have a lovely day." Jeremy hung up and set my phone on the table.

It rang again almost immediately. He set it to

Silent and turned it over to hide the screen. "I won't apologize. You don't deserve what she does to you, no matter who she is."

"Did you… You said…" I was focused on those three words.

Jeremy kissed the back of my knuckles. "That's what I wanted to talk to you about. I wanted to say it to you first, not her." He moved his palms to my cheeks and cradled my face in his hands. "I love you. For your mind, your heart, and your body. For the whole brilliantly sexy fucking package that's you, and no one had better fuck with you." He slanted his mouth over mine in a soft kiss that grew insistent in a blink, until he was devouring my gasp.

I dug my fingers into his arms to ground myself. To remind myself this was real. To keep him from slipping away. When he broke the kiss, he searched my face. "I don't want to hear excuses," Jeremy said. "I don't want you to tell me I'm wrong or I'm better off with someone else. I want you and him. I know it. I need you to believe it."

"I do believe it." And I was tired of pretending otherwise. "And I love you too."

Quentin cleared his throat. "Me too. I love you too. Just because he got to it first doesn't make me feel it any less."

I laughed, more to alleviate the huge bubble of stress and disbelief than out of amusement.

Quentin pulled me to my feet, gripped my hips

tightly, and brushed his mouth along my jaw. "Don't leave me out of this." His voice was quiet but there was power in his tone. "I'm not giving you up for anyone. I love you and I think I've loved you since the day I met you."

"Me too." I laughed at my own ridiculous response. Laughed through tears of disbelief and happiness and the confusion they were washing away. "I love you so very much."

Quentin picked me up, and I draped my arms around his neck, partly to balance me but mostly to hold onto him. I could get used to this kind of treatment.

Who was I kidding? I was already one hundred percent addicted to both him and Jeremy.

Quentin carried me into my bedroom and Jeremy followed. Quentin tugged up the bottom of my shirt, and pushed his hand back down.

He looked at me, one eyebrow raised.

"I think the two of you should get naked first," I said. "Help each other out of your clothes."

Jeremy grinned. "In case I haven't said so recently, I like the way you think."

"As long as everyone's clothes come off, I don't care." Quentin turned his attention to Jeremy to roughly yank Jeremy's shirt off.

"Slow it down. It's not a race." I wanted some seduction in my show.

Jeremy pushed Quentin's shirt up, kissing along skin and tattoos as he worked.

They helped each other out of their pants next, their cocks springing to attention. Quentin paused to stroke Jeremy until Jeremy's hips swayed in time with the motion.

Quentin pulled away and Jeremy gave him an exaggerated pout.

Totally worth watching.

But when they turned their attention back to me, the playfulness vanished in a hungry flurry of rough fingers on my skin and their mouths on my body.

Jeremy pressed his front to mine, slid his hands to cup my ass, and pulled me into him. I molded myself to his form, his erection digging into my stomach.

"On the bed, on your back," he commanded as he nudged me back with his frame.

I could be sassy and argue, but my anticipation was climbing and I wanted to see what happened next. I complied, loving the way both of them studied my naked, prone form.

Jeremy forced my legs apart and knelt between. Starting at one ankle, he kissed his way up the inside of my leg, licked along my thigh, and completely ignored the source of my need as he traveled back down the other side.

Quentin knelt next to us on the mattress and

lowered his head to suck on one of my nipples and then the other as Jeremy traveled up my legs again.

When Jeremy finally licked along my slit, a groan tore from my throat. He plunged his tongue inside me. *Goddess*, that felt incredible. But I wanted more. I tangled my fingers in his hair to guide his mouth higher.

Quentin chuckled. "Now I know why we restrain you."

"It's been a long few days. I deserve a little—"

I cut myself off with a moan when Jeremy wrapped his mouth around my clit.

"You really do deserve it." Quentin resumed lavishing my breasts with attention.

Jeremy licked and sucked, devouring my pussy as if I was a delicious delicacy. Combined with Quentin's skilled touch, I was squirming and moaning in no time. Grinding against Jeremy's face. Losing myself in the wash of pleasure that stole my thoughts. Fucking Hell these men could do incredible things with their tongues.

Orgasm came out of nowhere, sideswiping me and pushing me into a long scream that left my voice raw.

When Jeremy pulled away from my core, I collapsed on the bed with a breathless sigh.

This was better than a book or a movie or shipping fictional characters. Not just the sex—though that was incredible—but all of it. In this moment, captured between the men I loved, nothing had ever felt more right. I didn't know what I'd done to find such a wonderful thing twice over, but I couldn't imagine my life without Jeremy and Quentin in it. Having them, loving them, was better than perfect.

28 /
jeremy

I'd lost hope that I could have something like this feeling that burned inside me when I looked at Sonya and Quentin. It was the kind of passion I'd expected with Jenni, but that had never manifested.

It was here now and it was more intense than I thought possible.

As I pulled away from a flushed and writhing Sonya, Quentin tugged me back into him and kissed me hard.

Inspiration struck me. "I want you to fuck me while I fuck her," I said to Quentin.

His laugh of disbelief rolled through my back. "Pretty sure that's not anatomically possible."

"I promise you it is." And it was a lot of fun. "Do you trust me?"

"More than I thought was possible to trust another person ever again." Quentin's reply clenched like a vise around my heart.

I looked at Sonya. "What about you?"

"You have to know I'm in." Her smile was easy and bright.

"I'd hate to assume." I rested my hands on either side of her head, and she guided my cock inside her.

The way her lips parted in a silent sigh was the perfect accompaniment to her slick walls wrapping around me. I hovered my mouth over hers, and swallowed her gasp when I slammed inside her again and again, to memorize how she felt.

I pulled away enough to murmur against her skin, "Play with yourself. Make yourself come while I fuck you."

"I don't orgasm on demand," she teased.

"Maybe something to teach you." Quentin's voice came from behind me.

He spread my cheeks and I gasped when he slid a cool, lubed finger along my skin. When I was liberally slick, he entered me.

This was better than I remembered. Then again, this entire situation was new. Sure, there was orgy sex back in the day, but this, with these two incredible people…

No experience I had compared to the passion and desire flowing through us and connecting us.

Quentin and I had a few misstarts before we found our rhythm, and then we built to a fast pounding. Sonya tilted back her head and stroked herself as the three of us fell into a delicious synchronicity.

With the dual sensations enrobing me, it took the last of my restraint to not come. When Sonya spilled into climax, squeezing me tightly while Quentin moved inside me, I couldn't hold back. Orgasm pushed its way out, filling her.

With Quentin still hammering against me, my pleasure was drawn out, pushed to the limits of too much. He grunted and sounded as lost in the moment as I was. And then the entire room seemed to freeze.

And then he let out a series of short grunts, rocking both Sonya and I when he came. Taking his time slowing to a stop.

I wasn't sure how long we lay there, catching our breath before we untangled ourselves long enough to clean up. But dressing and getting ready for the day seemed like too much effort. We fell back into Sonya's bed, with her cradled between Quentin and I.

"You know what the two of you should do?" Quentin asked.

Lay here a bit longer and enjoy the lingering heat of some incredible sex?

"I know Jeremy should make a habit of doing that thing with his tongue. To me." Sonya's voice was pounds lighter than when she woke up this morning.

I loved her smile. Her light playful voice. So much of everything about her.

"I'm up for that," I said. "Or do you mean *right now*? Because I need a breather before I'm up for anything."

Quentin shook his head. "I did *not* mean right now, but I do think we should keep Sonya's idea on tap."

"Trust me—it's not one I'm forgetting, hmm… *ever*." Sonya played with a strand of her hair, brushing it over her skin, and trailing it along her fingers in a lazy path.

I was good with them discussing my oral skills on this scale. "You can have my tongue anywhere, anytime." I leaned into Quentin. "Same goes for you."

He gripped my neck, startling me, and pressed a thumb lightly into the side. The way he crushed his mouth to mine and probed deeper with his tongue fuzzed my thoughts and made my cock twitch.

When he let me go, a sigh floated from my chest. "You were saying?"

I swore the way Quentin chuckled was his equivalent of *I'm keeping that trick in mind*, and I hoped he did.

"You should make your own TV show, based on Sonya's book," Quentin said.

The color rushed from Sonya's face. "We can't…"

I liked the way Quentin was thinking, though. "Why not?"

"Jeremy is already writing a screenplay." Quentin sat up, excitement on his face. "There are fan films online that are TV quality, and the two of you have connections."

This was a fantastic idea. "We know digital animators, voice actors… So much of what we've done at work crosses into this." I'd be bummed this wasn't my idea, but I loved it too much to have any negative thoughts about it. "You put something together and then you start shopping a pilot around."

Sonya worried her bottom lip with her teeth. What was she thinking?

"We," she finally said.

Huh? "As in *oui oui*? Is that a yes?"

"As in, when *we* start shopping a pilot around." She looked up, her smile peeking through again. "The books may be mine, but the TV show is *ours*, and yes, that's a *yes*."

I let out a loud *whoop* and pulled Sonya into a long kiss. She was soft and pliant and having her this close made my blood hum. When I let her go, I turned to Quentin, and kissed him hard too. "That's for the idea," I said. "And really just because."

"Ah." Sonya's tone dropped. "I need to email Dominic and tell him I killed the contract with Epithet."

Now I had a brilliant idea. "Ask him if he can meet next week about this. Maybe he can act as our legal agent when we get back to negotiations again."

"Don't go anywhere." Quentin extracted himself from us. Watching him walk naked across Sonya's room without any hesitation was a gorgeous sight. He had the kind of toned body and grace that people wrote poetry about. Maybe I should write poetry.

He returned quickly and handed Sonya her phone.

When she looked at the screen, her happy expression evaporated. "Mom only called once."

"Does it matter?" I understood Sonya couldn't shed a lifetime of baggage in a few hours, but I wanted her to know it was okay to start.

She looked at me, head cocked to the side, and the corner of her mouth tugged up. "I guess it doesn't. Her reaction doesn't change how I feel about all of this."

"I'm happy to screen her calls going forward, if you'd like," I offered.

"It's okay, I can handle it." She squeezed my hand. "Though I may hold on while I do so."

I squeezed back. "I'm always here for that."

"But not today. Today we work on our plans." She muttered the occasional word as she sent Dominic an email, then dropped her phone on the comforter. "Sent."

Quentin tossed us each some clothing. Not a lot, but the T-shirts and shorts would keep our tender bits from getting too cold while we walked around the house.

"Come on. I'll make breakfast while you two make plans," he said.

In the kitchen, Sonya and I sat at the breakfast bar while Quenin cooked. We were coming up with a name for our project when Sonya's phone rang.

The clench of her jaw was obvious. Was it her mom?

She looked at the screen and let out a tiny sigh. "It's Dominic." She set the phone back on the counter and answered it on *Speaker*. "Hello."

"I'm sorry to call on a Sunday, but I just got your email so I figured the timing was good."

"No worries." Sonya sounded light and carefree.

"I'm glad you killed the deal with Epithet," Dominic said. "I wish you'd gone through me, but I'm more glad that it happened. You mentioned wanting to meet later this week. What about?"

Sonya and I explained the idea to create the TV show ourselves.

When we finished, Dominic chuckled.

I didn't like the sound of that. "Not at all the response we hoped for."

"It's not that," he said quickly. "I called because I spoke to Gabriel Groves. His goal is to attach his name to yours. It's not about the money, it's about his big return to Hollywood. And while normally I'd say that's a skeevy and to steer clear, I think in this case it could work in your favor."

"How so?" I asked.

"He's going to give you a lot of freedom and let you do most of the work, as long as he thinks it makes him look good. And you're going to ride the wave of his big return combined with Sonya's name. Honestly, I've played your game and the two of you have better odds of telling an incredible story than ninety-five percent of the people he'd bring on."

We chatted with Dominic a few minutes longer, our excitement growing, and he said he'd have his assistant schedule a real meeting for us soon.

Quentin set plates of pancakes in front of each of us, and saved one for himself as he stood across from us. "I feel like we should be having champagne or mimosas or something to go with this," he said. "To celebrate."

Sonya wrinkled her nose. "*Ugh.* No champagne or any alcohol ever again."

"Never?" Quentin's voice was flat.

"At least not until I forget how much this morning's hangover sucked."

I danced my fingers up Sonya's arm. "I can make you forget a lot."

"Such a big promise." Quentin still radiated disbelief.

Too easy. "I'm a big guy."

"You're not wrong." Sonya clucked. "But if I may say something?"

I gave her as much of a bow as I could from my seated position. "Always."

"Eat the food before you start talking us out of our clothes again. Quentin's pancakes are as close to sex as you'll get without it being the real thing.

That was a big promise. I took a bite, and "*Oh my God*," I mumbled through the best pancakes ever. I forced myself to not eat like a normal person, using the fantastic setting as a distraction. Watching Quentin smile and watching Sonya laugh...

This was love. Without question. I saw my future and my heart in Sonya and Quentin. I was going to hold onto it—onto them—for all I was worth.

epilogue

Six Months Later
Quentin

I'd been officially dating Sonya and Jeremy for a few months, and working out of Jeremy's garage just as long. After wrapping up the sculpture for Carly's client, another commission came in, and then another, until my schedule was full of people wanting me to weld sculptures for them.

It was amazing, but today I was taking a break to finish something else.

On days when I spent my time at Jeremy's welding and sculpting, he and Sonya came here after work. On the not-welding days, the three of us usually ended up at Sonya's. Regardless of whose house we went to, the three of us were spending the night together.

I finished my surprise while the sun was still up. Now what? I could get started on a different project, but I was excited to share this. This love I had with them was something I never thought I'd have again —never thought I'd want again—but there was no way I was letting it go.

Cleaning up my workspace only took so much time, and a shower took even less.

The unexpected sound of a car in the driveway made my heart leap. AcesPlayed was only a few months out from their official launch, and that meant a lot of long days and weekends for Sonya and Jeremy. To have them home in the afternoon was wonderful but strange.

A moment later they walked through the front door, expressions somber.

"Good. You're here." Jeremy's tone was flat.

"Hey." Sonya gave a short wave.

My excitement shifted to concern in a heartbeat. "Is everything all right?"

One corner of Sonya's mouth twitched up.

Jeremy frowned and nudged her.

She cracked, a massive grin spreading across her face. "Oh. My. Goddess. You don't even—I can't—"

"It's good news." Jeremy was smiling as well.

"So spill already." I had a few guesses as to what it could be, but I wasn't in the mood to go through even a short list to wait for the answer.

Jeremy bounced on the balls of his toes. "Your news. You tell him."

"*Our* news." Sonya looked like she was going to

fidget into another dimension. "We have a final contract for the TV show. Dom says it's solid, we're ready to sign."

"*Fuck* yes. *Woo.*" I let out a loud shout, and wrapped Sonya in a tight hug. They'd been putting in long hours on top of long hours to pull this nego-tiation and plan together, and to see them reach the next step was incredible.

With a tight hug and a deep kiss, I poured all of my joy for Sonya through the connection. "I'm so proud of you. I'm so happy for you." I gave her another kiss, then turned the same attention on Jeremy. They were Sonya's books, but he'd been as much a part of this next step as she was. "This is way better than my surprise. Wait." The rest of Sonya's words caught up with me. "*Ready to sign.* Why haven't you signed yet?"

"We don't want to hog the spotlight," Jeremy said as if they weren't about to start work on a fucking TV show. "What's your news?"

Seriously? "It'll wait."

"No, tell us." Sonya tangled her fingers with mine.

"And then we'll go back to celebrating your amazing news?" I asked.

Jeremy nodded. "Of course. I mean, unless yours is better."

It wasn't, but I did want to share. I led them out to the shed, and flipped on the lights to reveal a highly polished steel pyramid with a heart *floating* inside. It was suspended with a thin steel cable that vanished in most light.

"Happy anniversary," I said.

Jeremy furrowed his brow. "It's not—"

"Six months after we all pulled our heads out of our asses and said *I love you*?" Sonya approached the sculpture and reached out, but she didn't touch it. "It is. And this is gorgeous. Are those…" Her eyes grew wide and she hovered her hand over the three initials I'd created in a delicate script of raised steel. *S+J+Q.* "Our initials." She had one detail wrong, though.

"Yes," I said. "But it hasn't been said all around yet." The time never seemed right for me with Jeremy. Or rather, a sliver of lingering fear held me back, and I assumed it was the same for him.

It was time for me to let go of the pieces of my past holding me back, and move on to more wonderful things. I turned to Jeremy. "I love you. I never thought I'd be able to do this again, and now I have both you and Sonya, and I can't imagine my world without you in it."

"I love you, too." Jeremy yielded when I pressed my body to his. Gripped my shirt in his fists when I kissed him hard. Bit my bottom lip enough to sting then gave me an obnoxiously playful smirk.

There would be payback for that soon enough. "Now are you going to tell my why you haven't signed?" I felt light as air, having shared my surprise for them and saying what I wanted to say, but I was still missing an answer.

Sonya and Jeremy exchanged a glance that said she'd been scheming, but I was about to be let in on the details. She caught her bottom lip between her teeth. "The thing is, we need someone actually managing parts of this project. Dominic has suggested we create a formal production company and he has the paperwork ready for that, but we want someone else to join us."

"The being vague will only be cute for so long," I teased. And I was lying—she'd be cute regardless.

Jeremy held up his index fingers. "Ooh, ooh, ooh." He pointed at the heart sculpture. "We should use that. It would be the perfect logo."

"It totally would." Sonya clapped.

Though they hadn't told me yet what they were talking about, I'd put the pieces together. "Are you going to ask me, or just assume?"

"We want to work with you," Sonya said. "For all three of us to be a part of this company. You know as much about the books as we do now, and you've got the management skills from when you were contracting, and there's no one I trust more than you and Jeremy."

Despite knowing the request was coming, the words and the reality hit me hard. A business partnership. With the people I loved.

It was a terrifying proposition.

"If you don't want to, or if you want to structure things differently, I do understand." Jeremy's tone was even.

The furrow of Sonya's brow wasn't so neutral.

But I really was ready to move on. "I'm in. Let's do it. Three way partnership. Production company. Yes."

"*Yay.*" Sonya threw her arms around my neck. "I mean, if you'd said *no* I would've understood, but this is going to be so amazing. *Yay.*"

It really would be amazing, and I was looking forward to every moment of the rest of my life with these two incredible, brilliant, sexy people.

Jeremy

The noise level in the theater lobby was as epic as the event we were here for. Almost everyone from work was here, and so were Sonya's and my friends and family. The first three episodes of our TV show were dropping tonight at midnight.

Could we all be watching from our own homes? Sure. But this was a monumental moment and it promised to be even better if we watched surrounded by everyone we cared about.

Besides, this theater had been the first place to display Quentin's artwork—his sculpture was the main draw in the lobby—and that just added to how amazing tonight would be.

A sharp whistle cut through the room, and everyone stopped talking.

"Showtime in ten minutes." Dustin's voice carried.

Sonya squeezed my hand tighter, and with Quentin on her other side, I assumed she was doing the same to him. The last year had been a whirlwind of insanity as the three of us pulled this together. When Sonya and I weren't working on the game, we were doing whatever Quentin needed from us to make sure production stayed on schedule. Or our benefactor in name only. Or the streaming network that had signed us after seeing a pilot.

We'd seen the final, but this was different. Tonight was watched it with the world.

"Succeed or fail, this was worth it," Sonya said as we headed into the theater to find our seats.

"This won't fail." Quentin's self-assurance would have to stand for all three of us.

I believed in the project, so very much, but there was still that sliver of terror that no one else would recognize how great it was.

As everyone finished settling, the lights dimmed in the theater and the opening credits rolled on screen.

For the next three hours, we laughed and groaned and gasped and cheered, and everyone in the room did the same at all the right spots. By the time the show was over, I couldn't wipe the grin from my face and as the house lights came up, it was clear Sonya was the same.

"We did it." Her joy was almost tangible.

I pressed my lips to hers. "You did it. We just helped."

"No." Sonya shook her head "This took all three of us."

It took us more than an hour to get back to the lobby, with every person in attendance stopping us, stopping Sonya, to say how much they loved the show.

Yes, I'd done a lot of the screenplay writing, and Quentin kept the project on track, but this was Sonya's story. A brilliant creation from her mind. And it shone on screen.

But really, the most important thing to me aside from seeing Sonya get the recognition she deserved was that the three of us had come this far together —that I knew they were mine and I was here for them. That our lives were so perfectly intertwined and I didn't have to question if it was love or just friendship, because it was both.

And that regardless of what came next, our entire future spanned out ahead of us.

Sonya

I should be working. We had a story deadline coming up for the game, and the rest of my writers —except Jeremy—were working.

Technically I didn't need the job at AcesPlayed. My books earned enough to do more than pay the bills, and a huge studio had picked up and was currently creating the second season of the associated TV series.

But I loved my work. That, and I was an investor in the company now, so it was in my best interest to ensure the game continued to offer the stories players expected from us.

Instead of working, Jeremy and I were recreating a moment from a little over two years ago. Back then, we'd been refreshing the bestseller site, to see if I'd made my first ever bestseller list. Today, we were refreshing our email and staring at our phones, waiting to see if we'd gotten any Emmy nominations.

It seemed unlikely, but Quentin had worked with Dustin to make sure our series had the best possible chance.

And now we were at the mercy of the people who made the decisions.

Jeremy sat on the edge of my desk, supposedly distracting me but drumming his fingers as quickly as I tapped mine on the mouse.

It had only been a few minutes, there was no reason to hit *Refresh* again.

I did it anyway.

Emmy Nominees stared back at me from the screen, and it took my brain a moment to catch up with what the words meant. My phone buzzed and I ignored it.

"Are you going to look, or should I?" Jeremy's question jumpstarted my thoughts again.

"I can't." My stomach was a ball of knots.

He took the keyboard from me, hit the hotkeys to search, and typed in *Russel.* I almost stopped him —that was guaranteed to return Epithet nominations as well.

1 of 1 showed in the search box, and a name was highlighted in the middle of the screen.

I covered my face with my hands and peeked through my fingers.

"*We did it.*" Jeremy's shout made my heart leap. "Holy fuck, we did it."

Sure enough, there were our names, nominated for Outstanding Writing for... the rest of it all blurred together in a wash of giddiness and disbelief.

Luna's shout echoed through the building, and a moment later she had joined us, along with several other people from the office. Jeremy and I found ourselves caught up in a wave of handshakes and hugs.

This was all so surreal. How was I not prepared for this after all this time?

Because I wasn't, and honestly, I never wanted to lose this joy of amazing achievements like this. I accepted all of the congratulations, trying to memorize every one of them and sear this amazing feeling into my soul.

Jeremy and I took the rest of the afternoon off—it wasn't as if we were going to get any work done anyway, and we wanted to celebrate with Quentin.

He spent the afternoon plucking quotes from various entertainment websites about how fantastic our show was. How groundbreaking. Quentin also threw in the occasional headline about how this was Epithet's longest run without a nomination, people were starting to question Mary Russel's management of the company.

But mostly he focused on our show. The accolades. The positive press.

It was all great to hear, but none of it meant as much as the fact that I was celebrating this moment with Jeremy and Quentin. *My* happily ever afters. The men who supported and adored me, who I loved more than anything.

Without them, this wouldn't mean nearly as much, but with them, nothing was impossible.

Thank you for reading as Sonya, Jeremy, and Quentin tell their story.

There's more from the AcesPlayed gang in ACHIEVEMENT UNLOCKED. When Megan finds her fiancé balls-deep in her wedding planner, she calls off the wedding and swears off love. She's done waiting for the right guy to make her happy—she's going to discover herself in all of the things she's always wanted to do but was too terrified to try. Nigel is happy to help her out, and when they run into a friend of Quentin's, things really get interesting.